INFAMOUS HEART

MEN OF VANGUARD BOOK 1

RYDER O'MALLEY

MEN OF VANGUARD SERIES

<u>MEN OF VANGUARD</u>

Infamous Heart

Infernal Justice

Iridescent Light

1

———

"I didn't get the promotion," I mumbled to the table.

I dropped my bomb in the middle of banter about Alejandro's latest one-night stand, bringing the conversation to a halt. Cupping the large mug, the heat warmed my palms as I spun it about. The name of the coffee shop, Hideout, wrapped about the white ceramic cup. The spicy contents were already half gone when the call came in. I wondered if was possible to drown myself with only a half-filled cup.

Our table sat toward the back of the cafe where the only foot traffic was patrons heading to the bathroom. The three men grew quiet, seeming to stare off toward the black and white photography on the walls or the remaining croissant on the plate.

"Griff, they don't deserve you," Xander said.

"It's okay, guys." It was a lie. Nothing about that phone call had been okay. Not only had I not received the promotion, but Vincent had made it clear that I had reached my potential as a junior designer at the magazine.

"Fuck that," Alejandro spat. "I don't have an artistic bone in my body, and I can tell you're good at your job. I have some whisky in my bag. Need me to top off your glass?"

"It's seven thirty in the morning."

"My night is just getting over. Why should I be the only drunk one at the table?"

Bernard patted him on the shoulder. "What our misguided friend is trying to say, shake it off. They haven't respected you since you started working at the magazine. Maybe it's time to find a job elsewhere?"

The Hideout had gone from an empty coffee shop on the corner to the hopping destination every morning. Unlike the bigger chains, it maintained a homey feel. The wooden chairs and tables contrasted the white of the walls. It was a narrow space, dominated by the coffee counter where Chad slung drinks as quickly as the patrons ordered them.

This was breakfast club and the men sitting at the table had become my adopted family. After meeting Bernard, the hunky teddy bear, at the local dive bar, he had invited me to morning coffee. Now, our daily ritual included Alejandro dishing about his latest conquest in the bedroom and

Xander complaining about his job as a paramedic. Alejandro was getting off work from the nightclub where he tended bar while the rest of us were preparing to start our days. Lord knows I didn't need to be spending the money, but it was a fair price to see this trio of troublemakers.

Xander tore into his bagel as if it he might not eat for days. His manners were questionable on a good day, but as he spoke with a mouth full of cinnamon bagel, I could tell he was about to bestow some of his overly aggressive wisdom.

"Fuck. Them. You should quit. Alejandro can get you a job at the club. Or," he poked Bernard in the arm, "what about working public relations for the Centurions? Have you seen their graphics? Bernard's team could use somebody with your talents."

As usual, Xander paid a compliment and an insult in the same breath. Bernard rolled his eyes, a signature move that happened at least a dozen times when we met for morning coffee. Yet again, every person at the table questioned why they allowed Xander to join them.

"I mean..." Bernard started. Working for the premiere superhero team of Vanguard City, that wouldn't be a bad gig. Working at a magazine dedicated to showing the behind the scenes of superheroes had been a dream come true. It was like living in a comic book, and every once in a while, I had the opportunity to meet one in the flesh.

"I could talk to the bosses." Bernard played it cool, as if he wasn't referring to himself. His face hid behind his coffee as he slurped at the sweet nectar. It was hard knowing that the big burly man was, in fact, one of the Centurions, a superhero dedicated to protecting the Earth. Bernard believed his secret identity safe, a complete mystery to the world. I don't know about Alejandro and Xander, but I promised myself to never speak of it, not until Bernard was ready to come out of the spandex closet.

"It's okay." If I say it enough, perhaps I'll believe it. The entire situation was frustrating. I loved working for the magazine, but it was difficult to be the lowest man on the totem pole. "Maybe I'm just not cut out for the art director position."

It's Alejandro who interrupts my pity party. "If you're not going to believe it, then we'll have to keep reminding you." The three of them held up their coffee cups, waiting for me to join. They're the best friends a guy could ask for, and they would remind me non-stop until I caved. I lifted my mug in the air.

"Oh, what are we cheering?" Chad, the owner of the Hideout, had a knack for showing up when the gossip flowed. He grabbed a nearby chair and shimmied in next to Alejandro.

"We're celebrating Griffin getting his head out of his ass and realizing what an amazing guy he is." Thanks, Xander, I think.

"Speaking of an amazing guy... Griffin. Dear, dear Griffin. There is a gentleman who comes here in the afternoon that..."

"Whoa, whoa," Xander interrupts. "The last time you tried to set me up, they spent the entire date telling me about their mother's crochet hobby. Chad, you make the best coffee in town, but you are not a match maker."

"I don't know about that." Alejandro's smirk spread across his lips. "Last man he introduced me to, I wound up having a good time. Had the rope burns to prove it."

The coffee nearly shot out of my nose as I recalled the "morning report."

"Didn't he steal your wallet?" asked Bernard.

"It was worth every penny."

Chad rested a hand on my knee. Leaning on the table, his face softened, the beard almost looking out of place. "Seriously though, you're a catch, any guy would be lucky to take you home."

The alarm on his phone went off and he jumped up, grabbing a thermos from the counter. Everybody at the table held their mugs with both hands in preparation. The door to the coffee shop flew open, and a blur moved through the space and exited before the breeze caught up to him.

Zipper. The local super made a pit stop every morning at the same time. Why the fastest man alive needed coffee was beyond me. None of the patrons in the coffee shop looked up, accepting the fact that a man able to run Mach five had just picked up his daily intake of java.

"Not to change the subject." Alejandro was about to say something inappropriate. It was his only predictable trait. "Do you think Zipper is fast to the finish line in the bedroom?"

Everybody turned to look at the door. The question hung in the air and now it became a game. Who would break the silence to answer his question? I bet on Xander. Despite his dislike of superheroes, he wasn't a prude in the bedroom. I bet he thought—

"I'm more interested in how fast he's ready for round two."

Bernard saying something inappropriate? The burly man raised an eyebrow as he returned to his coffee. Alejandro's eyes darted to Xander, and me, shocked that the big man had joined in a racy conversation.

"Bernard," Alejandro whispered. "Have you," he checked to make sure Chad was out of ear shot, "hooked up with a Centurion? Basher? I can see you on all fours…"

The coffee shop filled with the sound of cell phones ringing. I reached for my phone and opened the Hero-App™. Thanks to working at the magazine, I had met plenty of superheroes, but it was always more exciting to see them in action. Several blocks away, a villain had broken into a warehouse. The app came in handy when deciding which streets to walk on my way to work. No point in stumbling into an alien invasion or a cyborg army trying to overthrow the government.

"Gentleman, it looks like I have to get to work." Bernard waived his phone. Whenever the HeroApp™ went off, it meant the Centurions needed him. "I need to make sure there's a statement ready when they blow up another building." He crafted the lies so well, I almost believed him. Bernard really needed to get to the secret lair, suit up, and protect the city. It was almost cute that he played average citizen.

"Me, too," Xander growled. Whenever superheroes went into battle, there were bound to be injuries. When a hero needed medical attention, it was up to Xander and his team to make sure they were bandaged and ready to go back into the world.

"While you suckers are at work, I have a date." Alejandro pulled out his wallet, leaving a tip under the mug.

"Of course, you do." There was no point in hiding my eyes as they rolled backward. "Just make sure this time they don't steal your wallet."

"Nothing left to steal," he thumbed through his wallet. "Maybe I'll try that trick and tie him up."

"And with that..." Bernard gave a wave as he and Xander exited the coffee shop.

"Oh, look." Alejandro inspected his phone. "Looks like Crimson Knight is responding to the alert."

I flipped to the detail screen. There was a little check mark in the top right corner, reminding me I had snapped a photo of the hero in action. The others mocked me for my love of superheroes and my determination to up my score in the HeroApp™.

"I never shagged a Knight." Alejandro did everything but lick his lips as he spoke.

Okay, so maybe I wasn't the biggest hero chaser amongst this group. My love of heroes didn't end with their capes on the bedroom floor as I added another notch to my bedpost. But to be fair, the Crimson Knight had a five o'clock shadow I wouldn't mind feeling—

"Ha!" Alejandro laughed as he got up. "You're thinking about it now, too. You haven't experienced sex until you've hooked up with a superhero."

Thanks, Alejandro. Now that image was going to be in my head all day. I guess it could be worse.

If the superhero showdown wasn't so far out of the way, I'd have taken a peek. I was only two superhero sightings from leveling up on the HeroApp™. It sounded foolish, but being a hero was a childhood fantasy. Unless I found a magical amulet, or sold my soul to a demon, spotting them in the sky was the closest I'd get to wearing a cape.

A flag above the comic bookstore whipped back and

forth in the wind. The giant "open" letters appeared and vanished as the breeze attempted to tear it from the holder. The storefront was fairly thin, perhaps a third the size of the coffee shop. New posters had been hung, providing teasers for a massive crossover event occurring later in the summer.

"Griffin!" Lydia waived a hand from inside the store, barely visible above the posters. Usually, I'd spend the rest of my morning debating the best hero, or most useless super power. After today's bad news, I really just wanted to wallow until I had to be at my desk. She detected my hesitation.

Cursing filled the comic shop, a cardboard cutout of a comic character toppling as she tried to speed past it. Lydia was hands down my favorite geek. Her recommendations always hit the mark, and her love of art warmed my heart.

"Don't act like you didn't hear me. Everybody hears me." This was a fact. "I have the newest issue of *Die, Hero, Die.* You're going to lose your mind when you get to—"

"Spoilers!" Yeah, she tended to get caught up in her excitement and give away the cliffhanger in every comic I purchased.

Standing just over five feet, she should be near invisible. The black t-shirt with a supervillain holding the severed head of a hero would swallow the average person. But the neon blue hair, gathered in pigtails, and the spiked choker, marked her as something other than average.

When she sped back inside, I followed. The smell of comic books bordered on arousing. Contained within twenty-six pages are endless possibilities. Once upon a time, I wanted to be a professional artist and create my own comics. Unfortunately, I also needed to afford rent and make sure my pizza delivery guy got paid.

"Is it wrong that I have naughty thoughts about Ricardo?"

Getting hot and bothered by a fictional character in a comic? Yes, but that made two of us. "I'd lick the sweat off his chest."

"You're nasty. I love it."

Lydia brought more pep into my morning than any amount of coffee Chad brewed. She yanked a copy of the comic from a box, scanned the barcode at the register and slipped it into the bag.

"Something's wrong." Her eyes narrowed, and I swore I could hear her rifling through the back of my mind. "There is a disturbance in the Force. Your dog is sick." At least I didn't need to worry about my comic shop owner being a secret telepath.

"No dog."

"Your mom forgot your birthday?"

"Not quite."

"The milk in your cereal went bad?"

"Strictly a toast guy."

"Oh, wait." Lydia's laugh bordered on a cackle. "That's

my morning. Your morning is your job not appreciating the work you do and you're thinking of quitting."

If Lydia had superpowers, the world was doomed. "How'd you know that?"

"Griff, you complain about your job all the time. It's not like I'm a psychic." With two fingers against her temple, she narrowed her eyes. "Or am I?"

I paid for the comic and backed away from the woman. "I'll read this tonight. Then we can argue which of us is getting Ricardo naked."

"I'll fight you, man. I'll fight you so hard." She turned to the box filled with custom orders, before spinning around, her eyes radiating a wild energy. "Then we can finish brainstorming our comic book. Don't think I've forgotten, mister."

I slid the comic into my messenger bag and stepped out of the store. The sun had turned up the intensity, promising another hot summer in Vanguard City. Only a few stores down, I paused, surprised to see the brown paper removed from the old candy store. There are few things that can make a graphic designer happier than the words, "Art Supply Store."

With time to kill, I might as well stroll down memory lane and recall my college years when I thought I'd be a famous painter. I traded passion for practicality. Usually, I'd be okay with this. But today, having been told yet again I wasn't good enough, I feared I had made the wrong choice.

I slipped inside, a tiny bell above the door jingling. The door hadn't even shut when I set my eyes upon a rack of sketchbooks. You're not an artist until you have a collection of empty sketchbooks falling off the shelf. Once upon a time, they were like a drug. My fingers dragged along the exterior, feeling the coarse bumps of the covers. It was good to see I hadn't entirely kicked the habit.

Turning the corner, the aisle held the canvases and acrylic paints. During school, not a single shirt I owned escaped the wrath of my major. It had been freeing, sitting outside, watching the waves along the beach as I tried to capture the essence of the shore.

I hadn't been a great painter, at least not skilled enough to make a career from it. But it seemed that was the story of my life: good, but not good enough. My ex had made it clear that I would never amount to anything. When he left me for a well-to-do investor, he cited that my goals weren't lofty enough.

"Oh...my...God," came a woman's voice. I spun. Being a large guy meant I took up plenty of room, and tight spaces like the aisle were my kryptonite. My messenger bag knocked several tubes of paint onto the floor.

"I'm so sorry." Add klutz to the mean things I'd say about myself today.

Near the back of the store, a woman in a long peasant dress held her hands over her mouth. For a moment, I thought she might be a classmate from art school, but try as I might, I couldn't place her.

"Sorry! I got excited. I didn't realize the front door was unlocked."

"Oh," I felt foolish breaking into the store. "I'll come back another time."

"No, no, no." She dashed down the aisle, kneeling and helping me pick up the tubes of paint. "Today is our grand opening. You're technically the first customer in my store!"

I held out my hand. "Welcome to the Ward, name's Griffin."

"Clarice," she shook my hand, her grip far stronger than her slender frame should allow.

"I guess if I'm your first customer, I need to buy something." The thick glasses exaggerated her eyes as they went wide and at the same time narrowed from the smile raising her cheeks. "What do you recommend for a former painter sorely out of practice?"

"In a few weeks, we're going to start having classes. I mean, if you're interested." Her nervousness put me at ease. This wonderful woman was attempting to carve out a spot for herself in the business world. Sometimes life throws you a lifeline when you're drowning.

"Where do I sign up?" Passion. This wasn't to put food on my table, or to validate my skills, it was purely for love. I could swear my heart thumped a bit in my chest. "I'll need to practice a little or I'll be finger painting."

Her arms darted to the paints, grabbing a tube of yellow, blue, and then red. She eyed the brushes before giving me the once over. Her fingers danced over the professional brushes before settling on a set of quality tools. "This is going to get you started. Do you need a canvas?"

"Oddly enough, I still have one in my closet. One of those projects you swear you'll get to someday."

She waived me toward the counter. "I don't want to sound desperate, but are you serious about signing up for the class?"

"I went to school for art. Life forced me into the design field. But," Not good enough, the thought hovered just inside the shadows of my mind. Despite my best efforts, I think I believed it. How could so many people be wrong? But art wasn't always about being good. "Yeah, I'm serious."

Lacking modesty, she performed a victory dance.

"You just made my day," she sang.

I paid and slid the paints and brushes into my messenger bag alongside the comic.

The dark cloud hanging over my head returned as I left the art store. None of these tiny victories could push back the sense of dread as I headed to a job reminding me every day that I'd never be good enough. A job that preached to the choir.

2

THE SECRET LIVES OF HEROES. IN A LARGE BOLD FONT, IT spanned the length of the room, just above the glass partitioned rooms used for the larger staff meetings. Since the writers had been given their assignments, the designers were left to take their ideas and collaborate with the photographers. Our mission was to create a magazine that jumped off newsstands and stood out on websites. I was one of those designers.

The Beacon occupied a three-story brownstone building on the edge of the Ward. Once upon a time, it had served as the office of a tech-start up, which made sense why my floor looked like a cubicle farm. The lowly designers and column writers occupied the same space as the distribution and sales folks. It made for an eclectic group of people in the break room.

It was easy to spot the designers from the salespeople. Known as the grotto, our cubicles were a smattering of interesting magazines and weird artwork we stumbled upon outside the Beacon. They were good folks to work with, and if I only had to deal with them, I'd be a happy employee.

The song piping into my earbuds ended. With nothing to do until the infamous Vincent approved my designs, I tried to look busy. I failed miserably, but at least I got to catch up on my podcasts and check out new music.

The bass riff started, and I spun about in my chair to see if any of my coworkers were about. Things were about to get incredibly weird in the design grotto. The tempo picked up, and it was impossible not to do a little head bob while mouthing the lyrics.

As the drums roll in, red pens transform into sticks. It starts with a light tapping sure to drive my neighbors nuts, but sometimes you just need to let the music take you. With a fast spin in my office chair, the beat pushes onward, building. The coffee cup serves as the snare while I tap my foot with vigor.

It's coming, the moment where the singer takes the stage. The earbuds go silent and I'm pretty sure Bob in sales is swearing. Sorry Bob, consider yourself lucky to have a front seat to the Griffin Smith extravaganza.

The singer takes to the stage, belting at the top of his lungs. Grabbing last month's issue, I roll it up, ready to make my debut. The chair can't contain this spectacle. Hopping to my feet, the chair rolled into the aisle. There's no doubt my co-workers believe I've lost my mind, and they wouldn't be too far off.

My dance moves are epic, and not in a good way. Far too many nights are spent watching music videos, and in the sanctity of my home, I unleash my inner freak. If I had hair, it'd be whipping side to side and there's a good chance I'd knock Janet's Troll doll collection from the cubicle wall.

Whoever thought gay men were born with grace and elegance had never seen this train wreck. But if I was going to sit through another day of having Vincent talk down at me, I was going to have fun in-between the tongue lashings.

I nearly jumped out of my skin when something touched my shoulder. My right earbud fell out as Janet pushed my chair into my cubicle.

"I meant to tell you, villain sighting this morning. I was in a taxi and this smoky woman showed up. It was intense. She was preparing to hurl my bus when Lady Liberty and Team Justice showed up."

"Lady Liberty, really? I still haven't gotten a photo of her."

I continued to shake my hips from side to side.

"Too late, I'm a level above you now."

I gave her a bump with my butt. "I'll catch up, just wait."

"While I enjoy," she waived a hand up and down my

body, "whatever this is, I'm about to ruin your good day." Nice try, Janet. My day started off ruined; nothing you could say could pull the rug out from under me.

"Give it your best shot, Lady Trollsalot."

"I'd choke you with my mouse cord, but I'm sure you're into that." Hostile, I expected nothing less. Our banter might continue for the next ten minutes as we attempted to one-up the other. Human Resources was at the other end of the room behind a closed door, and we took advantage of the distance.

"The spread you did," her voice softened, almost to a whisper. This was going to be worse than bad. I dropped down in search of my earbud as she continued her story. "I was upstairs meeting with Carlos, that super-hot photographer we've been sending to do the home shoots. The guy is a genius, I really think with him in charge of the photography, the magazine will move to the top shelf. It doesn't hurt that he's— "

"You're killing me! Get to the end."

"I listen to you rattle on about men all the time. Suck it up."

She had a valid point. "Fine, go on."

"That's it. He's hot. What more do you want, pervert?"

She might be my work wife, but it might be time for a divorce. I'd let her have the kids, I'd keep the plants. We'd go our separate ways.

"Back to the Holo spread."

"Oh right," I loved her, truly, I did. "Vincent had your spread, and he was presenting it to Bossman. It seemed he was quite the fan of your layout. Bossman used words like, 'visionary' and 'revolutionary' as he looked it over."

My heart swelled with pride. "Really?"

"No. But he said he thought it was a great artistic direction for the magazine. He wants to see more work like that, and it looked like we were all about to be your underlings."

Here it came. "Looked?"

"Vincent took credit for your work. That asshole outright said your concept, the design, everything but the execution was his. The Beacon Devil strikes again."

It was one thing to reject me, to say that you didn't believe my ideas were strong enough to lead the design team. All morning, I raked myself over the coals, questioning my worth. Vincent had reached into my chest and squeezed my heart and forced it to stop. But for him to send me on a downward spiral and then take credit for my victory.

"I'm going to kill him."

Janet leaned out of my cubicle, checking that the door to Human Resources remained tightly shut. "If you need to dispose of the body, I have some ideas."

I knew she was joking… I suspected she was joking, but I nearly wanted to take her up on the offer. The despair that clawed at me all morning vanished in a blaze of anger. There was no point in going to Vincent and having the man try to back pedal his way out of the conversation. It was time to put an end to this.

"I'm going to speak with the Bossman."

"Fine." She straightened the neon pink hair of a troll doll that sat on the divider between our cubicles. "Let me know if I need to Google acid delivery companies." After I talked to the owner of the magazine, Janet and I would need to discuss her anger management.

But first...

3

―――――

"I will destroy you."

The mysterious man's voice penetrated the walls of Bossman's office. I waited in the lobby area outside, leaning over the desk of Sofia, his personal assistant. Her eyes lit up and I could tell from the panic, the meeting taking place was not going well.

"Who is in there?"

I set my story boards on Sofia's desk. Vincent might be able to steal credit for my individual designs, but that moron couldn't speak his way around all my hard work. Armed with the best spreads I had produced for the Beacon, I believed I could put my talent on display and, at the same time, stop him from taking credit for the designers' work. His villainy ended today.

Sofia leaned to the side before dropping her head to

dish. This week, she had bleached her hair, adding streaks of pink that stretched from the tips until her shoulder. It was the least crazy thing she had done with her hair since the mohawk catastrophe. It was rare I came to this floor unless it was for the quarterly report meetings, but Sofia never shied away from gossiping.

"Damien Vex." Her voice was so low I could barely hear her. When I didn't give her the reaction she expected, she stole another glance at the door. "He's the owner of Revelations."

The reality of our newest competition in the office with Bossman set in.

"Ohhh. What is he doing here?" I whispered. "Why would you meet with your only rival?"

The man's voice lacked any civility. "Good intentions be damned. I will ruin this antiquated rag!"

It had a bit of a snarl as he threatened Bossman. Part of me wanted to ensure that our owner wasn't being threatened, but I always wanted to glimpse a man bold enough to threaten somebody in their workplace.

"I'm going in."

The space outside his office wasn't large, a few steps, and I was on the edge of the glass panels that framed the door. He could have drawn the curtains, but Bossman hadn't seen any need for privacy.

Inside the spacious office, the magazine owner sat at his desk, calm, as if he were meeting with one of his staff members. In one of the two chairs facing the owner, a man jumped up, leaning forward so I could only make out his black suit. He attempted to intimidate Bossman, but it didn't seem to be working. If only he would... They weren't alone.

To the side of the desk, a man with his hands crossed at his waist waited for the tantrum to end. Much like Damien, his black suit was tailored to highlight the narrow waist and broad chest. It only accented the pink dress shirt underneath and the unfastened top button. The dark shadow created by his short beard framed his jaw, making it appear even more angular.

"Who's with him?"

"What?"

Sofia, I demanded gossip, and I needed it fast.

"The man with Vex, who is he?"

"Contrary to popular belief, I don't know everything that happens in Bossman's office."

The sculpture of perfection barely moved as Vex and Bossman traded more words. I nearly tripped over myself as the owner stood, gesturing toward the door. I dashed to the desk, trying to hide my guilt.

"Smooth, real, smooth, Griffin."

Feet stomped across the lobby to the door leading toward the elevator. I held my breath as if sucking in oxygen might somehow draw attention. Sofia flipped open an appointment book and started running her finger along the page. "I'm pretty sure we can squeeze you in next week." It wasn't her first time playing innocent.

"Let me leave Mr. Vex's card in case Mr. Bossman reconsiders his offer."

He was only two feet away, but I couldn't turn my head and make eye contact. I doubled down on my efforts, frozen as if I might be reading the schedule upside down.

"Thank you." His hand entered my peripheral holding a black card. Sophia quickly accepted, and he stepped around me as he exited the room.

"Give me that card." I was too slow as she leaned away, out of reach unless I wanted to mount her desk.

"What's it worth to you?"

"Did you see him? He might very well be the sexiest thing to walk the Earth. Hell, even his cologne."

"Just his cologne? That's the sexiest thing?" She couldn't possibly understand. It'd sound clichéd to mention my heart skipping a beat or butterflies in my stomach. No, it was the sultry quality to his voice that left me wondering how it'd sound first thing in the morning.

"His voice." It was warmth. "I want him to whisper in my ear."

"Did you catch his smile?"

Sofia's questions were awkward, even for her. Then the hair on the back of my neck stood on end. I had been duped.

"He's not standing behind me."

Sofia wouldn't receive a Christmas card from me this year.

"Mr. Sexiest Man on Earth, is there anything I can do for you?"

If I didn't turn, it wasn't real. Even as he cleared his throat, I refused to accept I had just made a fool of myself in front of him. It was time to prove that the universe ignored allotting me my share of game.

"I'm so sorry, I—" I knocked my story boards across the floor. I couldn't decide if it was more or less embarrassing if I ignored the obvious mistake. I opted to crawl on my knees and pick up the boards.

The sexiest man on Earth dipped to one knee, grabbing a piece of cardboard covered in color swatches and sample layouts. Standing, he inspected my work. It was bad enough that I made myself appear to be a love-struck puppy, but now he scrutinized my designs.

He stepped closer, hand extended. "Mind if I see the rest?"

Don't speak. Don't say anything. You're an idiot and there is only so much shame you can muster in a single day.

"Yus." Did I just fail at saying yup? Wow, Griffin.

"You're not afraid of letting the color rival the photography. The headline treatments, are they period inspired?" I nodded. I couldn't screw up nodding. I hoped. "The spread for Zipper, that's genius. The way you incorporated elements of speed into the typography, it feels electric."

The sexiest man alive complimented my work. I smiled, fearful my mouth would get me in trouble. Asking to sniff another human wasn't quite socially acceptable.

"This is outstanding. The Beacon is lucky to have you on the staff." He reached into his pocket and produced another card. Handing it to Sofia, a smile spread across his face. Oh God, the butterflies they were alive and flapping.

"I should have left my card as well. Sebastian Taylor." He might be standing across from Sofia's desk, but his eyes were firmly locked on me. "In case you need to get a hold of me to discuss..." His voice trailed off as she snatched the card, annoyed that the hottest man in the room wasn't focused on her.

"You're welcome." Ugh. I'm never going to speak again.

Sebastian slid the storyboards to the stack in my arms. It was near impossible to focus on his face as I stared at the chest hair around the first button of his dress shirt. Did it travel all the way down? I restrained myself from stealing a glance at his package.

"She has my number. Call me," he said. With a wink, he exited once more, leaving me to dissect every stupid thing I had done.

Sofia held out the card, her electric pink nails pointing at the bottom. Balancing my work in one hand, I yanked the card from her. The small print read, "Revelations

Artistic Director." If ever I had experienced tragic irony, it paled in comparison to this moment.

"I'll make a copy for you," she said.

"What for? It's not like he meant it. It's the polite thing to say." None of what I said made sense, but could this hunk really be asking me to call? Was it work related, or was it personal? Did I care either way as long as I got to see him? There was something taboo about the man, the art director for the Beacon's only competitor. It felt naughty, even for me, and I have to admit, the tightness of my pants enjoyed the thought.

"You're hopeless. Griffin Smith can't tell when a handsome man is flirting with him. I don't know what to do with you."

I was about to speak when she pointed to Bossman's office. He had situated himself behind his desk and waived me inside. It was hard to focus on my argument about Vincent and his lack of management skills. Instead, I wanted to daydream about the softness of Sebastian's beard.

One problem at a time. "Wish me luck."

4

―――――

"I SEE." BOSSMAN HELD ONE OF MY STORYBOARDS, DIGESTING the immensity of my words. "You're telling me that Vincent had no involvement in these?"

"Well," I straightened out my back, determined to feel like a member of the Beacon community. "He isn't doing anything *for* the magazine."

"You're sure?"

I nodded. For the last twenty minutes, I explained my designs in and out. Bossman didn't have an artistic bone in his body, and relied heavily on the staff to fulfill the magazine's mission. While he had no artistic talent, he appreciated our work, to a point.

There was a long pause as he inspected the boards. Seconds dragged into minutes and I feared I'd overstepped professional boundaries. Several times I caught myself, ready to break the silence. Even if it didn't end well, I stood taller, knowing I had made an argument for myself.

"Mr. Smith," he moved the boards, carefully stacking them. "I have no doubt that you're a talented young man. You've done the superhero community a service with your work. I fully acknowledge that our magazine wouldn't be successful without the journalists, photographers and designers."

The "but" hung in the air.

"Did you know I'm a legacy? My father ran a magazine, and his father ran the largest newspaper in Vanguard. I've been surrounded by people with far more talent than I could ever muster. So, if I can't write tear-jerking pieces or snap photographs that bare a person's soul, what do I bring to the table?"

"Your business expertise?" He might not have the ability to execute his magazine, but he did have a vision. Bossman understood what the people wanted and delivered. The readers loved the behind the mask approach of the publication so much that heroes actively tried to appear in our pages.

"I want my creative team to push boundaries. While you're reinventing the Beacon with every issue, it's my job to manage and rein in the creativity. I believe us suits are necessary to make sure the magazine doesn't descend into chaos."

He held up a finger while picking up the phone. "Ms. Hahn, send Mr. Bailey in."

I gulped. It was one thing to see Bossman to discuss an idea, but for me to go over my supervisor's head, I had reached beyond my position. Instinctively, my shoulders slumped, and I tried to shrink to avoid the impending confrontation.

No, not this time, not for this jerk.

I straightened my back and watched as Vincent strolled into the office without a care in the world. He should be the one worried that somebody was spilling his dirty secrets. Not once did the crooked smile falter. Vincent had been taking credit for our work for so long he believed himself untouchable.

"Mr. Smith here has made some allegations about your oversight."

Vincent didn't bat an eye. With how poorly he managed the staff, it was a surprise this hadn't been brought to light before. But knowing that it meant he was either extremely good at avoiding scrutiny, or he was an incredible liar. It was definitely the latter. The man thrived on confrontation.

"Has he? Griffin is a fine employee, I can't—"

"You're a waste of a paycheck." The words left my mouth before I could parse them into something with a professional tone. If I was about to get fired, I might as well finish by saying my peace. "You've created a hostile work environment on the second floor. The creatives do all the work. Time after time, you sit back in the meetings and have us pitch ideas, and then you claim you came up with them. You're taking credit for our work."

"I am the artistic director."

I laughed. "Artistic? You provide no direction to the magazine. We've been driving the ship since you got here. If we didn't respect one another, you'd have us putting trash on the newsstand."

"Where is this hostility coming from?" As I spiraled, my face turning red with anger, he remained calm. "Is this because you didn't receive the senior designer position?"

"Don't turn this around on me."

"Like I said on the phone. You're a valuable member of the team, but you need more experience managing creatives. Perhaps in a year or two, when you have the respect of your peers, you'll be ready."

Perhaps Vincent had a point. I could always use more managerial experience, but—I growled. I wish I had recorded the conversation to point out the inconsistencies in his story. This wasn't about a bad boss. The man attempted to gaslight me, and I continued to fall for his guise of sincerity.

"It seems there is a miscommunication about the roles of each position. Mr. Bailey, you would do well to better oversee your staff. Mr. Smith, you—"

"No. This isn't about positions or titles. Mr. Bossman, I care about this magazine. There's nobody here with more love for the superhero community. Vincent is going to alienate your talent and without us, the Beacon is doomed."

"Mr. Smith," the man leaned forward on his desk, resting his elbows on the glossy surface. His fingers laced together as he carefully picked his words. "Are you giving me an ultimatum?"

Locking eyes with Vincent, I forced my lip down, hiding my grinding teeth. I didn't come into this meeting worried about losing my job, but it had quickly taken a turn.

"As a businessman..." The Griffin from this morning would have backed down and shied away from the confrontation. Normally, I'd have said my apologies and taken my lashes, but something in my chest burned. Was this self-respect? "As a businessman, you have a decision on the table. It's him or me. Eventually, it'll be him or the rest of your staff."

"Griffin, I'm sure we can find a way to improve your skills for the next time the position opens." Vincent couldn't help himself, the need to salt a fresh wound.

"Have a wonderful day, Mr. Bossman."

With that, I turned around and left. My career had been carefully set on the chopping board and I expected by the time I reached the lobby, I'd be unemployed. Already, the conversation replayed in my head as I dissected each statement. I'm sure once I reached the street, I'd regret every decision, but until the self-doubt dragged me under, I'd celebrate my dignity.

"I respect you so much right now."

"Thanks Alejandro, I think."

"Griff, this guy has been walking all over you. He deserves to be fired. You're like a superhero at the magazine."

The park had become our regular hang out after work.

We indulged in our love of street food while people watching. Joggers squeezed in a late run while moms pushed strollers gossiping about their days. The splashing of the water fountain offered a bit of serenity in an otherwise busy city.

While I wrapped up my workday, Alejandro was just crawling out of bed, preparing to head to the night club and begin prepping the bar for a wild night. As I dipped a piece of pretzel into a tiny paper cup of mustard, it dawned on me that Alejandro was wearing the same clothes from breakfast.

"You didn't go home, did you?"

Alejandro stuffed his face with a steak and cheese sub, mumbling as he did. None of us were prudes, but Alejandro had a knack for finding himself in a different bed every night. Working at a nightclub that specialized in superhero clientele meant he often had the freakiest hookup stories to tell.

"Powers or not?"

He shook his head as he swallowed. "Nope, just a good ol' fashioned blow and go. No super strength, flying, or invisibility. But who knows what tonight—"

"I met somebody." Since Dan and I broke up, most of my dating stories ended with a punchline. While Alejandro had a new fling every night, I couldn't remember the last time I had gotten laid.

"Stats." Why was I not surprised he wanted a visualization before I continued?

"Dark hair. Short, trimmed beard. About my height. His shoulders were broad and the suit he wore..." I whistled.

"Boxers or briefs?"

Alejandro and I had plenty of weird games we played to pass the time. Sitting in the park, boxers or briefs had become the most popular. Find a sexy man and then debate on what he wore underneath. With how many men he managed to get naked, I was playing out of my league.

"Bikini briefs. Contour pouch." The thought of Sebastian in nothing but dress socks and underwear would be masturbation material for later.

Before he could ask for a follow up, our phones vibrated. The trio of women power walking around the fountain took out their phones. This was a common occurrence, and gave away the HeroApp™. Every phone came with it installed, an early warning system for when the powered community was about to partake in a battle. When the women picked up their pace, running from the park, I fished out my phone to see the proximity alert.

"Oh, looks like we'll get a show today." Nobody has identified the villain or hero yet. I hope it's somebody new. I might finally level up on the app.

"Anybody interesting?"

It takes a minute before the icon appears with the villain's profile. "It's Wraith again. She seems to be everywhere lately."

I stuffed the last of the pretzel in my mouth, savoring the salty, gooey dough. Out of nowhere, a man flew past, nearly within arm's reach. I managed to snap a photo as he dodged the water fountain.

"Cobalt. Drats." The Ward's hero frequently made appearances at the coffee shop. Of all the heroes I had met, he was one of the most down to Earth.

"Hush," Alejandro said. "I'd watch that man pick up litter."

"I need two more photos."

"Do you get extra points if they're naked?"

The term "hero chaser" didn't quite cover his determination to conquer heroes. Everybody said I was the biggest superhero fan in our group of friends, but I think they neglected just how much Alejandro liked being teleported as he orgasmed.

A massive black sphere swallowed Cobalt. There wasn't much information about Wraith, but she wouldn't stand a chance against a veteran like him. Whatever shadowy ability she wielded, it paled in comparison to his telekinesis. Readying the camera on my phone, I waited patiently for the villain to emerge from her trap so I could snag a photo.

"Boxers or briefs?"

"Who?"

"Cobalt," Alejandro said. "I'm betting commando. I think he's the type who gets excited by the leather on his junk."

"You're projecting," I laughed. "He's a boxer brief guy. It mixes the flexibility of boxers and holds his cock in place at the same time."

"I'd hold his—"

"I wish I had your confidence." Maybe not that much, but enough to feel confident to talk to a guy. I did great in social situations, but the moment I thought a guy was cute, I stuttered and threw my story boards all over the floor.

"When Bernard first brought you to breakfast, I was annoyed."

My face scrunched up at the new information. The three of them had been nothing but welcoming. We were close now, but to know it wasn't always the case stung.

"First rule of breakfast club?" he fished.

"Bros before hos?"

"Second rule, then." Alejandro poked me in the arm, grinding his thumb into my shirt.

"No shagging the members of breakfast club?"

"There you have it."

Each morning, it seemed we added more rules to the list. In the past week we'd added, "Thou shall not spoil episodes of Criminal Superheroes" and "Members must point out poppy seeds stuck between teeth" and of course, the most important, "No making fun of Bernard's mustache." But it had started with three:

1. Fuck buddies cannot join Breakfast club.

2. Do not sleep with members of Breakfast club.

3. Honesty above all else.

My cheeks turned red, and I pretended that something interesting was happening at the end of the park. The fact our second rule irked him... did he find me attractive? Alejandro could very easily have any guy at the bar, and often he did, sometimes all at once. I was flattering myself if I thought somebody like him had once thought about adding me to his list of conquests.

"So, we're just going to ignore it, interesting." He shimmied closer on the bench, wrapping his arm around my shoulders. He was going to make it awkward. "You were the cute new kid on the block. I was going through my slut phase back then."

I started to question the "back then," but he moved his hand to my head, pulling my cheek against his shoulder.

His palm covered my mouth, ensuring I didn't ask him about the hearts he broke between breakfast and now.

"Anybody would be lucky to wake up next to you. I know you don't believe it, so I'll keep reminding you. But for the record, I would have rocked your world."

I pulled his hand away and gave him a kiss on the cheek. While I'm sure it would have been the best sex of my life, I was grateful we skipped straight to the best friends stage.

"For the record," I poked him in the thigh. "I would have wrecked you." His eyes lit up at the statement. "You'd have limped for days. You'd scream my name every time you came."

"Damn, Papi." He gave my hair a playful rustle. "I guess I got lucky."

I jumped up as Cobalt's body shot out of the black sphere. The superhero sailed closer. Alejandro followed suit and grabbed my arm, tugging for me to follow. The hero had gone limp as he approached the fountain. A streak of black followed, gaining on the man.

"Safe distance." The voice came out of nowhere. The scenery shifted so fast, my stomach took a moment to catch up. When it did, I fought to keep myself from hurling. Alejandro, on the other hand, lost the battle and hurled into a nearby bush.

"What," he wretched a second time, "happened?"

We were a few hundred feet from the fountain. A silver

blur caught Cobalt and set him down on the same bench we had just been sitting. For all the times I had seen the Zipper running in and out of the Hideout, I had never actually been saved by the speed demon.

Wraith approached, waves of dark energy cascading from her hands. I raised my phone, taking video of her hovering high above the fountain. Zipper slowed, a rare sight, eyeing the villainess. I hoped he gave her a solid punch to the jaw, a fair return for knocking Cobalt out of the fight.

What kind of abilities did she have? Could Zipper outrun her? Were we safe? The kid in me rooted for the heroes, wanting them to save the day only to receive applauds of the onlookers.

Wraith flew straight upward, far out of the reach for even Zipper. Without Cobalt to launch him upward, he couldn't reach her without buildings to run up. I took a deep breath, thankful it didn't get any worse, even if it wasn't the epic battle I hoped for.

Faster than my eye could track, Zipper gathered his unconscious teammate and vanished. I switched over to the HeroApp™ and posted my video of the confrontation. One more super powered being, and I'd finally level up.

"Somebody," Alejandro hurled again, "kill me."

5

THE CURSOR OF THE LAPTOP BLINKED. THERE. GONE. THERE. Gone. Each time it appeared, it taunted me and my inability to focus. There. Gone. It had been years since I sat down and wrote a real resume. Need somebody to balance the color of throw pillows, I was the guy. A website that said, "look at me," sure. Hell, I could cite the overabundance of Flemish painters and their obsession with tiny hands. But a resume? Not so much.

I leaned back on the couch, staring at the ceiling. I hadn't done bad for myself at the Beacon. I lived on my own, paid my bills, and had enough money left over to buy a couple rounds of beer. There was enough money in my savings to pay next month's rent, but beyond that, I didn't have a plan. I wasn't sure I was going to be fired, but I might as well prepare. I'm Griffin Smith, and I live in a world of worst-case scenarios.

There. Gone.

"Saved from a supervillain, but defeated by a resume. I hope they put that on my tombstone."

I slapped the laptop shut like an infant having a tantrum. There were so many other things I could be doing right now. I hadn't taken a nap in months. Maybe it was a hobby I should explore? My foot brushed against the messenger bag. Forget reality. There was an epic storyline I needed to see through in *Die. Hero. Die.*

The cover of the comic served as the finale to series, and they spared no expense. Thick card stock paper, glossy cover, ultraviolet embossing? It would be amazing to work on a project like this, to experience this level of freedom. The artist had Jacob Short, the invincible *Hero,* falling to his knees, bits of his shredded costumed balled into each fist. I could only hope it served as an allegory, and that by the end, Hero would save the day. Angst and brooding were well and good, but only if, at the end, the hero stood victorious.

I peeled back the cover. *Whoosh.* The alert meant an email awaited me. Could it be ignored? I lifted the phone, staring at sealed envelope on my lock screen.

"If I got fired, my night is ruined. If I didn't get fired, my night is still ruined. Just do it. Like a band aid. Do it."

Despite my award-winning motivational speech, my thumb resisted.

"Stop being a coward." I swiped. I focused on the giant still life of the Eiffel Tower I had painted in college. It had hung crooked on the wall for so long, it appeared as if the structure was slowly sliding off the canvas.

I glanced down, then back to the painting. This was no different from easing your body into the cold water at the pool. First toes, then feet, step out, then back in. The dance took far longer than necessary. But either way, eventually the water touched your junk, and everything shriveled.

"Ter..." The tablet on my coffee table needed to be charged. The windows, covered in smudge marks, needed to be cleaned. Hell, I couldn't recall the last time I vacuumed the rug in the living room. A million other things distracted me from the confirming the rest of the word on my phone.

"Terminated. Effective immediately."

There was no point in reading. Standing up for myself had felt empowering at the time, something I wish I had done years ago, but this is where it landed me. If I had knuckled under, kept my mouth shut, and let Vincent take the glory, I'd still have a job. It would have been miserable, but at least I'd have a paycheck. Now, it was misery without pay.

"Griffin, what did you?"

Opening the laptop brought a new sense of dread. If I

couldn't get a new job soon, dating weirdos would be the last of my worries. I grabbed the phone and stared at the group text message. If I told the guys, Bernard would offer a comforting bit of advice, Alejandro would have a sharp comment, and Xander would threaten to beat them up. I appreciated their love, but none of it changed reality.

Sitting next to the laptop, a black rectangle screamed for attention. The embossed silver lettering sank into the paper, demanding a thumb to run across the textured paper. I had only met Sebastian this morning. Was there any truth to the grace period before reaching out? If I contacted him, would he see me as needy? Did dating protocols apply to business?

"Screw it," I picked up the card. Revelations had spared no expense with something as simple as their business card. If they spent money on something like this, it boded well for how the company functioned on the interior. Even Mr. Bossman's business cards came from a cheap printer, a red flag if there ever was one.

I could call the man, and the thought of his deep voice did have its appeal, but the coward in me took the easy route. I texted him instead. Nope, delete that, too desperate. How about something casual? Oh, for Christ's sake, no, that sounds like we're besties. Delete. Delete.

"Hey, it's Griffin. We met earlier today at the Beacon. Would love to talk business with you." Love? Too strong?

Would he remember me? I was about to delete the text message when my clumsy thumb hit send.

"Shit."

Three seconds passed before I eyed the message. Why hadn't he responded? Did I creep him out? What if he ignored strange numbers? What if...

"Griff, you're going to drive yourself crazy. People have lives. Breathe." My logical brain did little to calm the growing list of questions bombarding me. It was the adult equivalent of asking the popular kid to prom.

A distraction. I needed something to take my mind off my crumbling life. Reaching for the television remote, I hit the power button, prepared to drown myself in the Food Network.

"This is the third Wraith sighting in as many days. The supervillain's goal is currently unknown. This afternoon, she managed to overpower Cobalt in the Ward. However, she didn't persist as Zipper arrived on the scene."

The footage played. "Hey, that's my video! Stupid reporters swiping my content. I deserve a shout-out."

They zoomed in on the woman as the reporter cited the growing number of villains appearing in the Ward. The contour of her body gave away that she was a woman, but she was nothing more than a black silhouette of a person. Hidden in the shadows of her face, two bright white orbs shone against the darkness.

"Living shadows, great, nightmares come to life. Just what we need."

Usually villains were robbing banks, holding up stores, or hell, securing deadly chemicals to turn the city into zombies. It was par for the course, and we all accepted the new normal as if it weren't insane. But this villain, she didn't destroy ATMs, rob the food vendors, or even give a speech about her plans for world conquest. Something about her was even more unnerving than the scientist turned evil spider.

I jumped as the phone vibrated in my lap. Unlike before, there was no hesitation. I needed to see what he had written. I was going to be pissed if it was another meme from Alejandro.

"Would love to talk and look over your portfolio."

Stay calm. Be cool. Give it a minute like you might be doing something other than pining over a text message from a sexy man. I counted to three before texting. I started to respond, let him see the three dots. Nothing he could say would make my day any worse.

"Drinks. Tonight?" The three martini glass emojis left me smiling. Funny how a simple icon can defuse the tension.

"Time and place?" See, I can be cool.

I hadn't been into the downtown area of Vanguard City in years. Our secluded borough across the bridge maintained its quaint personality while being progressive and affordable. The city proper, however, was genuinely out of my price range and the moment I saw the prices on the drink menu, I remembered why I stuck to bars like Bottoms Up.

"Your work," Sebastian turned the page in my portfolio. I stupidly brought the oversized book. It would have made more sense to bring my tablet to show off my work. As he eyed the images up and down, I hope he didn't think I was one of those antiquated designers.

"It's excellent. You have a great eye. I can see when you take a backseat to let the photography and article shine, but your best work," he turned to a previous page, "is when you say screw the rules. There's a risk taker hiding in there."

In one statement, he paid me more compliments than Vincent ever had. He reached for his whisky, twirling the amber liquid in his glass before taking a sip.

Much like Sebastian's drink, the Marigold was a swanky restaurant. The trio of candles in the middle were real wax, not the type with batteries. Even the bartender wore a dark vest and dress shirt. As I eyed the other patrons, money oozed from watches, earrings, and fancy clothes. I realized I had come underdressed. Jeans and a superhero t-shirt didn't quite say, "I belong in the Marigold."

"You look uncomfortable. Is everything okay?"

How do you say I'm out of my league? "I'm used to slumming it in the Ward." I pointed to the logo on my t-shirt. "You city folk, too rich for my tastes."

Oh good, insult the man who picked the location.

"You look just fine to me." Wait, did he mean fine, or did he mean *fine?*

"You're handsome, too." Meeting men was so much easier when it was a blind date and your expectations were low to begin with. But knowing this man was handsome and successful, and maybe into me... it made things *complicated.*

Sebastian laughed. "Handsome? I'll take that. But I admit, it's adorable watching you panic. You don't go on a lot of dates, do you?"

"Date?" The tables had turned. "You're handsome, but a date? I think you'll need to buy me a drink before it's a date."

Somewhere, Alejandro cheered my attempts at being suave. "Okay, you caught me. Your portfolio is great, honestly it is. I'd have asked you out at the Beacon if my boss hadn't threatened your boss minutes before."

"*Former* boss." If we were going to be honest, might as well put it all on the table. "I stood up to my art director and got fired for it. Teach me to grow a backbone."

"Vincent? That idiot? He might very well be the reason why Revelations dominates the market. You did the right thing."

"It's great to have morals, but they don't pay the bills."

He finished his whisky and held the glass up for the bartender. The man in the vest nodded and started another drink. Without delay, a waitress delivered the booze, swapping it out with the empty glass.

He pointed to mine. "Refill? Since I'm buying you a drink, after all."

"Margarita, no salt. So, what is there to know about the mysterious Sebastian Taylor?"

"I'm an open book. What do you want to know?"

"Where'd you grow up?"

"Southland." This tall, dark, handsome man came from the roughest part of Vanguard City. The tiny area south of the docks had a reputation for being dangerous. Back then, it was known as gang territory and not much had improved since.

"My grandparents were Italian immigrants. My Nonno knew people in the old country. You'd call them mobsters, but they were just trying to flee the Lon'eta Invasion. Those cybernetic aliens did a number on the country." He took a sip as the waitress slid my margarita on the table. I quickly sipped it through the slender straw.

"We didn't have money. We were always one bill away from being undone."

It wasn't the story itself, but how he told it. He broke eye contact as he described his grandfather and his work ethic.

There was a sadness in voice, as if traveling down memory lane might be tougher than he let on.

"In fifth grade, we went to the Metropolitan Museum in New York. Some big company sponsored the poor kids. Have you been?" I nodded. "The painters could see past the world in front of them. There were some strange things, strange and *amazing* things. I wanted to be like them and see more than drug deals happening on the corner of my street. So, imagine my parents' surprise when I told them I wanted to be an artist."

"It's nothing but fame and fortune. I'll have to invite you to my summer chalet."

"But you know what?" he held up his glass in a salute. "I showed them. Poor scrawny kid from Southland is kind of a big deal these days. I haven't looked back since. Southland can rot. I got out and plan on keeping it that way."

"So, you never go back?" I asked. "Not even to see family? I'm sure having a living success story would be an inspiration."

He chewed over the words. I had unknowingly pushed my way into dangerous territory. I didn't try to understand the relationship he had with his birthplace, but I could tell it wasn't a good one.

"I make my donations to the high school. They tried to do right by me, but never had the resources. They'll have to make do without my presence. Can we switch topics?"

A slight bit aggressive, but who am I to judge? I held up

my glass, toasting to his good fortune. "How did you wind up at—"

"No, no," he protested. "It's your turn. Mr. Smith, where are you from?"

"I grew up just outside of Portland, Maine. That's about as exciting as that story gets."

"Don't sell yourself short. How'd you get from there to here?"

A woman in a fur coat walked by. She waited patiently for the host to assist her from her jacket before pulling out her chair and helping her get seated. I didn't want to judge, and I especially didn't want to balk at Sebastian, but I lived the bohemian lifestyle. I didn't ask for anything in life, mostly because I tried to enjoy it as is.

"Loaded question. I won a few art contests in high school that put me on the radar of the New School in New York. When I applied, I received a scholarship and a work study package that I couldn't resist. I technically have an art degree, but I didn't see how to make money with it, so I took a few design courses and wound up in the corporate world."

"Seems we both found our passion in New York. But why Vanguard City?"

I laughed at the question, reaching for my drink. I would need more tequila for this. "It's embarrassing. It really is."

"I still play with Legos."

I spit the drink into the glass. "Wait, what?"

"I have the Millennium Falcon in a glass case in my office. I'll deny it if you ever tell anybody, but I got it as a gift last Christmas from my Nonna and we spent the day putting it together. Can't be more embarrassing than that."

If I kissed this man right here, would anybody care? If he spent as much time on his grooming as he did his clothes, I could assume his beard would be soft against my face.

"Superheroes. Vanguard City has more superhero sightings than any other city in the United States." I chugged the rest of my drink. "I'm a comic book geek." It might have become more mainstream with the number of superheroes running around in their leather uniforms, but it still came with a stigma.

"Legos and comics. It sounds like we need to have a play date."

His euphemism hung in the open, while I stared at the open top button of his shirt. The dark chest hair underneath teased a hairy torso, but not so much that it would hide the contour of his muscles. The table hid my erection as I imagined the buttons tearing off his shirt.

"We can save that for the second date."

"Second?" Why did I keep acting like it was impossible for this hunk of a man to be into me? Come on, Griff, you can play his game.

"You bring the Legos, and we'll have a slumber party."

Okay, not my best line, but I think it deserved an A for effort.

He scooted to the edge of his chair, crossing his arms on the table. His tone shifted from playful to serious. Could I have offended him? Did he not like to share his Legos?

"Since you asked me here to talk business, let's finish that and then you can decide if you want a second date."

Underneath the light banter and obvious sexual tension, Sebastian transitioned back into business. Was he worried that I only invited him out for his connection to Revelations? I had never experienced an office romance and feared I might have intermingled my personal interests too deeply into my professional life. The moment I thought about it, I fell down a rabbit hole of self-doubt.

"I like your work, but Mr. Vex is extremely hands on. I can give him a recommendation, but he'll want to talk to you himself. I can get you an interview, but it's up to you to get the job."

Instinctively, I reached across the table, resting my hand on his arm. The moment I touched him, I froze at the realization of what I had done. "I want to be clear," I eyed my hand, "*This* has nothing to do with a job."

Instead of responding, he moved his arm. I had violated the man's boundaries. It was dumb. This is what I get for channeling my inner Alejan—he rested his hand on mine, his thumb running circles over my knuckles.

"Good," he said, "cause getting you a job has nothing to do with how much I want to see your comic collection."

Swoon.

The night was young, and we were suitably tipsy. While there was a list of things I wanted to do to this man, I decided to keep my hormones in check, at least for the moment. Instead of running back to his city apartment, which I'm sure was far ritzier than my own, I wanted him to see the type of guy he was courting.

"Street food? Really?" We had sipped cocktails at a restaurant that offered bottles of wine that cost more than my paycheck. Now, I dragged him toward the theater district to my favorite post-pub-crawl street food.

"You'll never eat a pizza this good. You need to trust me." I tugged on his arm, standing in line. The small service window was like a fast-food drive through, but instead of cars, the line was filled with people heading to the clubs or business men who had to stay too late at work. There were suits next to crop tops and accessories, including brief cases and spiked collars.

Unlike the fancy place where we started the night, this was nothing more than a parking lot facing flat buildings. The only thing that broke up the walls of brick were alleys and the occasional rear entrance. Lando's pizza remained a well-kept secret, but that didn't seem to hurt the business.

"I can't remember the last time I ate pizza," he mused.

"Are you even human?" A single statement explained how different we were. There was no denying we came from different sides of the tracks. Knowing he came from a humble beginning meant there was common ground somewhere in there. "You didn't have street food in Southland?"

"We had the street market, but my Nonna insisted on us eating at the dinner table."

The line moved quickly and before he could back out, I ordered him a slice of the house special. He reached for his wallet, and I put an end to that. "On me. Besides, when it changes your life, I want all the credit."

Once the paper plates slid into reach, I handed one to Sebastian and off we went to wander while devouring pizza. We had just cleared the parking lot, heading into the showier part of the district, lined with brilliant marquis when, I heard Sebastian swear.

"What's wrong?"

"This pizza." he had a mouthful, but didn't let that stop him. "It's amazing."

I folded my plate in half and savored the smell as I stuffed my mouth. Whatever prim and proper manners Sebastian had, they vanished as he shoveled in another mouthful.

"It's like sex on a plate."

I couldn't argue with the assessment. If sex with Sebastian was half as good, I'd be a content man. As he tipped his head back, moaning in an obscene manner, I imagined him naked and me on my knees making him moan like that. Maybe I *should* suggest we head back to my place.

A nearby marquis, lined in bright flashing lights, dimmed until the light vanished.

"Did you see that?" I asked.

"Is there a black out?" The wave of black rolled forward, sending the street into darkness. A few people leaving the theaters pointed, but most ran, knowing what was coming. I might not be a superhero, but I recognized weird, and thanks to my obsession with the HeroApp™, I knew the likely culprit.

"This way," I pointed to a nearby alley leading away from the street. "It's Wraith. I saw her take on Cobalt and Zipper earlier."

There were no terrorized screams or people going into hysterics. Everybody had received "Villain Preparedness" training at some point. We lived here knowing the risks and, just like a fire or earthquake drill, we immediately went into action. It wasn't as if every villain wanted to murder people, and if they did, what were we going to do to stop them?

I fumbled for my phone, hoping somebody identified Wraith's destination.

"Griffin."

Sebastian worked at a magazine that revolved around people with powers, he must be used to this ritual. I wondered, did Southlands have as much superhuman activity? I froze as my phone vanished in a ball of darkness, growing until my hand and forearm were swallowed.

"Griffin, we need to run."

I turned just in time to see a black blur strike Sebastian, hurling him against a dumpster. The metal bent under his weight before he slumped and rolled onto the dank alley pavement. I wanted to yell, to make sure he was okay, but my words were caught in my throat as the black tendrils snaked down the building.

Every geek has imagined what they would do in a time of crisis. We believe we'll bare our knuckles and go down kicking and screaming, but reality is cruel. The soles of my shoes were cinderblocks, and my arms remained locked in place. For a moment, I wasn't sure I controlled my body.

"What do we have here?" The voice matched her powers, a breathy hiss that echoed off the narrow space.

"L-l-leave us alone." It was the best I could do. The darkness blotched out the night sky and the remaining lights from the flashy signs on the street vanished. Even though I couldn't see it, my phone bounced off the concrete, the sound ricocheting off the walls, louder than should have been possible.

"Where are your heroes now?" She dragged out the "s" in heroes as if it were a hiss.

"They're coming." My muscles tensed, preparing for the inevitable sting of her shadowy limbs. Were her powers less about the darkness and more about smoke? The air smelled as if something were burning nearby, a gross synthetic fragrance that forced the nose to scrunch up.

Wherever she hid in the shadows, she sniffed the air. She smelled it too, so it couldn't be from her. But if not from her—

"He warned you."

A bright white light cut through Wraith's darkness. I traded one blindness for another. Massive orbs of iridescent purples and blues filled my vision, and I couldn't make out what was happening. Had one of the heroes arrived? Who had light powers? There were too many to count.

Reaching for the alley wall, my foot caught on something, sending me toppling to the pavement. First rule of superhero battles, get to safety. In the tight space, there wasn't far for me to go, so I scooted against the wall and tried to tuck myself into a ball.

"Who are—"

It was a brilliant white light. I couldn't make out details, just one flash, then another. It would have been the same if I stared at the sun at high noon. It didn't help narrow down the potential heroes. There must be a dozen within a hundred miles that possessed light related powers.

A woman let loose a blood-curdling scream. Despite shielding my eyes, the rapid switch from dark to bright created more orbs. I thought I could see a black shape slam against a fire escape. Had the hero won?

"This isn't over," she hissed. The shape vanished, consumed by the orbs in my vision. I couldn't tell if she flew away or merely teleported. Either way, I was glad to see she wasn't going to use me as a hostage to secure her victory.

As she sped away, the cloud of darkness vanished. Replaced by a radiant light, I had to hold my hand up to shield my eyes. It was a man composed of light, tiny orbs hovering about his body, popping like bubbles as they drifted away.

"Are you okay?"

I rubbed my eyes, and when I looked again, the searing rays vanished, leaving a regular looking man. No, scratch that, leaving an incredibly sexy man, one who had confessed to playing with Legos.

"Sebastian?" I couldn't believe it. "You're a hero?"

"I wouldn't go that far." He held out his hand. Without any effort, he pulled me to my feet. Only inches from my face, I could see the milky white of his eyes, tiny shimmers creating a strobe effect.

I put a hand on his chest, surprised he had torn open and discarded his dress shirt. Not so much surprised, I guessed; a bit elated.

"You rescued me." Disbelief. The sexy man who had flirted with me over drinks and experienced his first slice of Lando's pizza, he was a superhero? My geek dreams had come true.

"I need to get you home."

"So, you can chase Wraith and save the day?"

"I don't care what that crazy woman decides to do with her night." He fished around for his suit jacket, buttoning up his shirt while I stared like a kid at the candy store. Taking my hand, he escorted me from the alley. Once on the street with the theaters, the people returned, moving to their destinations for the night.

"I'm anything but a hero."

Not to me, Sebastian.

6

———————

I CAN'T TELL IF THE IMPOSSIBILITY OF SLEEP WAS FROM THE thrill of nearly being killed by a b-list supervillain, or discovering the secret identity of a superhero. The taxi ride from the theater district, across the bridge to the Ward had been a silent one. I didn't want to pry, and he hadn't offered any explanations.

As we walked toward my building, he finally spoke up. "Please," he begged, "don't tell anybody."

I swore to keep it a secret, but in truth, I didn't know what I was keeping a secret. Did he not want the world to know he had powers, or did he not want his secret identity put on display? The questions were piling up, and quickly I spun myself in circles.

With that, he dropped me off at my apartment, gave me a hug with a kiss on the cheek, and left. My mind was reel-

60

ing, and I didn't have the bandwidth to question why it ended with just a friendly peck. Had I been in my right mind, I'd have ignored his superpowers and invited him up for coffee. If all went well, it'd have ended with breakfast.

For the first hour, I sorted through every hero on the HeroApp™. Light Lord? Too skinny. Storm King? Twenty-years too old. Blue Bolt? Not cyborg enough. Despite running through every hero, none of them matched the physique of Sebastian Taylor. Were his powers new? My mind continued to race with questions.

I had decided to take that nervous energy and do something productive with it. Sitting at my easel, mixing paints on my palette, reminded me of why I loved art. I funneled all these questions into the anxious brush strokes. What started as an urban landscape similar to the streets of the theater district, pivoted to painting the dashing man who saved me.

It started with the black and white suit. When it came time to start mapping out his face, it only seemed logical to use Sebastian as my inspiration. When he transformed, what usually happened to his clothes? Did he fight naked? There was something hot about imagining him nude, but more so wielding this ethereal energy while he remained exposed.

The painting was a long way from done, but if I stayed up any later, I'd never get out of bed in the morning. Not that I had a job demanding punctuality. I dropped the brushes into a mason jar filled with muddy colored water. Rolling my chair away from the canvas, the painting was looking pretty good for my first attempt in years. His clenched fist needed more definition, and the lighting came across as flat, but I found myself satisfied.

"Sebastian has powers." It still wasn't processing. The statement threatened to make my head implode. Instead, I opted for something I could wrap my head around.

"Dear God, he's into me."

Sebastian had an air of confidence about him; not quite cocky, but enough if he wanted something, he'd go for it. It was obvious that he was good at it, or how else would he have gotten the art director position? Creative and handsome, it was a dangerous combination.

"Why the hell are you into me?" I asked the replica of him on the canvas, shocked that it didn't respond to the question. "Why the hell *are* you into me?"

I had been so caught up with Sebastian and his powers, my geeky curiosity washed aside my romantic feelings. He had everything he could ask for, a career, plenty of money, and an attitude that probably kept him balls deep in men.

On the flip side, I was jobless and only a month away from being broke. Hell, even if I had kept my job at the Beacon, I was a nobody in the grand scheme of things. Was Sebastian one of those guys who slummed it with a nobody to feel better about themselves? If Wraith hadn't spoiled the evening, I could have been on the receiving end of a pity fuck. Not the worst end to a night.

"Man, you are so far out of your league," I mumbled.

Dan had left because I couldn't measure up to his standards, and he was an average guy. How would I ever be able to compete with Sebastian, to play on his level? I knew the answer, written in stone and unchangeable: I couldn't.

"At least I gave it a shot."

I yawned, my body informing me it was long past my bedtime. After a quality night of sleep, I'd meet with the guys and see if any of them had job prospects. First, make sure there's money to pay bills, then I'd deal with the train wreck that was my love life.

I made my way to the bedroom when I noticed the blotches of paint on my favorite superhero t-shirt. A splatter of black paint covered the chest of Captain Jack. Careful not to cover myself, I stripped the shirt, balling it and setting it on the dresser. Seconds later, I laid naked in bed, watching the ceiling fan lazily spin as if it had some place to go.

Obsessively, I replayed each interaction with Sebastian. From Bossman's office, to drinks, to the alley, I couldn't shake that grin from my mind. How sexy would it look in the dim light of the moon coming in my window as he kneeled over me? The image of him straddling my torso, his bare chest...

I threw back the blankets. The thought of Sebastian

riding me was enough to get the motor going. I reached down, surprised at the speed I went from soft to rock hard. I pinched the foreskin, covering the head of my cock. I don't know why men pretend they'll touch themselves for a few seconds and get on with the day. The moment I touched myself, it was a lost cause. On a good note, it was the fastest way to guarantee I got a solid night's sleep.

I wanted him kneeling over me, so that when I looked up, I could admire the dark coating of hair covering his chest. Having seen him without his shirt, it confirmed my suspicion that it trailed all the way to his navel. A man that concerned with his appearance would be clean shaven, and his package would sit on my chest, waiting for me to tip my head forward, my tongue licking the tip of his shaft.

The thought of his cock inches from my mouth could have sent me into an orgasm, but I wanted to savor the image. Wiping my finger across the head of my cock, I spotted the glimmer of precum. I licked my finger, hoping he tasted as sweet.

He'd slide a hand behind my head, lifting it until his cock touched my lips. There'd be that smirk as he pulled his hips back, keeping it just out of reach. And when he was good and ready, tired of teasing, he'd finally give in. He'd pull me close, his other hand bracing on the wall as he slid the length of his cock in my mouth, pushing into the bend of my throat.

There were few things as hot as having a man fill my

mouth, pumping his hips. While he face fucked me, I'd be holding onto his hips. As he got close, I'd reach back, cupping his ass, forcing him as deep as I could manage as he—

My toes pointed downward, calves and thighs tense, as I tried to both ward off my orgasm and ride the wave. My cock throbbed as the warm sensation pulsed through my groin. An instant later, I could feel the pressure build, and cum dribbled along my hand down the crook where leg joined to the groin. I let out a long sigh, surprised just how rigid my body had been. Now, it was as if the bed had softened and threatened to swallow me whole.

I should take a shower, partly to wash away the mess, but also scrub the acrylic paints from my arms. I settle on a middle ground and grab a towel off the floor and wipe myself down before running my fingers across my skin, checking for any missed wet spots.

Spent and satisfied, I tucked my hands behind my head, letting my eyes sag. Out the window, the moon hung high overhead, the light filling my room. What if Sebastian hovered outside my window, his cape fluttering in the breeze? What if he...

7

———————

"Griffin should key his car."

The Hideout's customers were coming and going in droves as patrons snagged a quick coffee before heading to work. Chad had mastered the art of pausing to connect with his patrons before moving like a madman to ensure drinks continued to appear on the counter. It wouldn't be long before he dropped a thermos full of coffee on the bar for our local superhero.

Alejandro dismissed Xander's suggestion. "No, that's too obvious. He needs to do something downright sinister. What if he looked up his boss's dad and shagged the man?"

Bernard rolled his eyes. He sipped his coffee before pointing at the two men. "Arson? Revenge sex? No," he chomped on the bacon, his face the definition of bliss. "Find his dad, marry him, then show up at Thanksgiving dinner wearing a t-shirt that says, 'Who's your daddy?' That's a proper revenge."

Alejandro and Xander mulled over the idea while shoving breakfast in their mouths. "Bernard," I scolded, "what have we said about egging them on?"

"Bernard's the real evil genius." Alejandro blew the burly man a kiss, earning him a brief smile. "Even if you don't burn down his house, you're better off. Nothing good was going to come from that place."

They were wonderful friends. What is it the kids say, my ride or die squad? They'd have gladly stood by my side at trial or raise bail should I opt for arson. But try as they might, they didn't understand what it meant to have the only entry point for my career slammed in my face.

No matter how bad it got, I knew Bernard would let me crash in his guest room until I got back on my feet. Alejandro would use his social circle at the club to find me position. Hell, even Xander would... okay, so Xander wouldn't do much unless I wanted him to punch Vincent in the face. I'd have to take a rain check on assault, at least for the moment.

"I want to revisit the rules," Alejandro said between bites of toast.

"No," Xander said. "He fucked the guy twice, and now he's convinced it's love. No. Not just no, but hells no."

Alejandro's bottom lip pushed out in an attempt to sway the argument with his pouting. A cell phone alarm sounded and everybody in the coffee shop froze. The bell jingled. A blur entered, grabbed the coffee and vanished just as quick. I should be elated that a superhero had graced our presence, but the Zipper had become a staple of the Hideout.

"What if he's the one? My forever love!"

"Forever until one of those damned supers offers to rail you while flying over the city." Xander had a point. Alejandro tended to drop everything the moment a superhero showed interest. But who was I to judge? I had unknowingly crushed on a superhero.

"You're suspiciously quiet today," Bernard said. He narrowed his eyes. The burly man's gaze was reading me while he sipped his coffee. Try as I might, I couldn't help but smile. His hand slammed down on the table. "I knew it!"

"Knew what? What did I miss?" Xander followed the man's steely gaze. It took a moment before his eyes widened, a smile spreading across his lips. "Griffin, you have exactly three seconds to tell us everything or we banish you from breakfast."

"I don't know what you're—"

"Hogwash." Bernard might know me a bit too well.

"Did you just say that? Hogwash? How old are you, Papi?" Alejandro had a knack for saying what we were all thinking.

"Honesty." Invoking the rules, Bernard? Really? That's

not fair. What if I wanted to keep my crush on Sebastian a secret? All three were focused on me, frozen, until I gave them a juicy morsel to wash down breakfast.

"I had a date last night." The words came out quickly. "And it was good."

"Is he good in bed?" Alejandro might need to start attending meetings for sex addiction. "Above average? Did he spend the night? Which nipple does he prefer being pinched?"

"Let the kid talk," Bernard smacked Alejandro on the shoulder. "You know we're not leaving until you tell us."

He'd risk his job for this showdown. I should be unnerved by their persistence in violating my personal space, but there was a reason. The way they were still, muscles tensed, they physically prepared to cheer if it went well or console if it didn't.

"He didn't spend the night." I swore they leaned in as if I were whispering secrets. "But I like him."

"Second date?" Xander's question set me back in my chair. After nearly being killed by a villain and finding out Sebastian wielded light like a weapon, we hadn't really talked about a follow-up.

"Oh, I'm so sorry." I jumped at the sound of Chad's voice. The barista had been hovering behind me, listening to the conversation. He had a knack for always being present when we discussed dating tragedies. "They can't all be winners."

"It's not like that. I originally met him to talk about a job opportunity. He thought it was an excuse for the date and was a little shocked I brought my portfolio."

They all leaned back in their chairs, shaking their heads. Leave it to them to judge my naiveté.

"But then the flirting started. I—We had a moment," I concluded.

"Rule number seven," Chad rested a hand on my shoulder, giving it a squeeze. "Never end a good date without scheduling the next."

Shit. That made sense. I think it was obvious that I was into Sebastian, but without confirmation, did he think the night was blown? I assumed he had been dwelling on outing himself as a superhero, but perhaps he wasn't into me? Oh, God, this quickly spiraled out of control.

"Ignore Chad," Alejandro said. "His marital bliss has softened his dating advice." He flashed a smile at the barista.

"Don't let these vultures intimidate you." Xander pointed at the three men, scowling. "But really, Griff, you can't say you had a moment without telling us."

"Legos." It was comical to think that something so juvenile had been the moment that gave me butterflies. "He plays with Legos."

If I had said it to anybody else, they would have laughed, or thought I was being a fool. A man playing with a children's toy would set off red flags, a massive warning that the man hadn't grown up. But they knew my obsession with superheroes, and they'd spent hours with me in the comic bookstore going through back issues. They raised their coffee mugs in a salute. These were my people.

"That deserves a coffee on the house." Chad gave me a quick hug before darting behind the counter to deal with the barrage of customers.

"It sounds like you need to set up a second date." Bernard clanked his mug against mine. "You deserve it, Griff. We need somebody in this group to find some serious love. Maybe then these two wouldn't be such jaded bitches."

I spat my coffee into my cup. Bernard had a knack for being reserved, but when the claws came out, he struck with precision. While Xander and Alejandro should be angry with the man, they both nodded in agreement.

"Do you think he'll let you play with his Legos? And just to be clear, by Legos, I mean his penis."

Leave it to Alejandro to skip the romance. I wanted to give him the finger. But after lying in bed last night, fantasizing about Sebastian, naked in my bed, it was on my mind. As he so delicately put it, I wanted to play with Sebastian's Legos.

My phone vibrated in my pocket, giving me the perfect opportunity to dodge the question. I held up my finger as I fished for the phone. Blocked? It was probably a telemarketer, but on the off chance that Sebastian might be calling, I answered.

"New rule," Xander said, "no phones at breakfast."

"Vetoed." Alejandro shook his head. "I might get a booty call. You know, important bar tending business."

"Vetoed," Bernard checked his phone. "Centurions saving the world trumps breakfast."

They continued to rattle on, arguing over the rules of breakfast, for which there were always too many. I turned in my chair, holding the phone to my ear.

"Is this Mr. Smith?" The voice had a deep timber, almost sultry in how smooth the words rolled out.

"It is. May I ask—"

"It's Damien Vex. Sebastian Taylor phoned this morning to discuss a meeting he had with you last night." The man's voice bordered on accusatory. I couldn't quite tell his feelings about my drinks with his art director.

"Oh yeah, he looked over my portfolio."

"He believes you're quite a talented man, Mr. Smith." I bit my lip, thankful he couldn't see my face turning red. "From the superheroes we feature to the staff I employ, my business revolves around talent. Are you available to meet?"

"Uh," This was happening faster than I could have hoped. "I mean, absolutely, Mr. Vex. I'd be glad to discuss opportunities at Revelations."

"I trust Mr. Taylor's instincts, but I take a great deal of

care knowing my employees and the skeletons in their closets."

"I understand. Thank you for the opportunity." Truth be told, it sounded more like a police screening than an interview. The man had a confident manner, but it was hard to ignore the subtle threat. Did he know about Sebastian? Was that his meaning? My mind reeled with the possibilities.

"I have availability later today. I'll have my assistant reach out to set up a time."

"Thank—" The connection ended before I could respond. In true fashion, my mind darted through the conversation, picking apart every word in an effort to better understand the situation.

Turning to face the table, they had moved onto Xander, sharing another disgusting story from the back of his ambulance. We should not be friends with him. His stories had far too much blood and, when he added sound effects, my breakfast struggled to stay put.

Chad had refreshed my coffee, and I quickly took a sip. "Hate to interrupt your missing leg story, but *I* have a crush on a sexy man. That's right, Griffin Smith's love life isn't dead. And if that wasn't a good way to start the morning, I also have a job interview."

"He's going to be insufferable now," Xander laughed.

"That's worth celebrating." Bernard raised his mug again.

"Get the job first, then I'll buy you a cake." Xander had a point. Nothing was set in stone, but I didn't care. After being hung out to dry by Vincent and the Beacon, things had taken a drastic turn for the better.

"I'm glad to see you smiling like an idiot," Bernard said.

Me too.

8

UNLIKE THE BEACON, REVELATIONS WAS LOCATED IN A BUSY part of Vanguard City's business district. The magazine had taken over the top three stories of a skyscraper, complete with penthouse. Revelations had only been on newsstands for a few months, quickly challenging, and surpassing, the Beacon. Their owner, Damien Vex, seemed to have no problem flaunting his money. It meant he could afford generous salaries, which boded well from an employment perspective, but the audacious way the man flashed his wealth struck me as obnoxious.

The Beacon occupied a brownstone, fitting into the quainter Ward. Here, the metal and glass couldn't be any more downtown if it tried. I walked in the door to see the lobby was just as grand as the exterior. It had a water feature in the middle with benches scattered across the wide-open space. People were having late lunches, socializing, and appearing to enjoy themselves. I could get used to this type of treatment.

I walked past the water fountain, admiring the bronze sculpture of a Roman warrior clad in armor holding the Earth between his shoulder blades. Before I reached the receptionist standing behind a marble white counter, Sebastian appeared from the elevator to the side. He quickly signaled to the receptionist that I was with him, and she gave a quick nod.

I hadn't expected him to greet me in the lobby. But as he sauntered across the large space in his black suit and blood red shirt, I grew excited. Despite knowing he had abilities making him different than the average person, I was excited to see Sebastian Taylor, the dashing man.

"We need to talk."

These were words that no human wanted to hear. With four words, every muscle in my body tensed, causing my fingers to tighten until I nearly bent my tablet. Studying his face, I searched for contextual clues. Would this be an unfortunate situation where he expressed he wasn't interested? Had Vex sent him to ward me off after reconsidering my employment.

He kissed me. A stolen peck on the lips, far more intimate than anything I had imagined. Muscles relaxed as I scoured the lobby, looking for anybody staring. Even the slightest bit of intimacy in a public space made my heart flutter.

"About last night," his voice grew soft, barely a whisper, "nobody can know."

"Know what? That we met for drinks, and you walked me home like a gentleman?"

The worry on his face melted, his broad shoulders shrinking in his spiffy suit. Whatever speech he had been prepared to give, the begging to keep his secret safe, it vanished. While his brain tried to wrap around my nonchalant acceptance, I found his insecurity humbling. This man had all the power in the world at his disposal, and yet, a single secret could break him.

"Oh," I teased, "you're talking about when you tried to kiss me, and I said not on a first date? Yeah, that was awkward, but you're going to need to work for it."

Sebastian rolled his eyes even as a smile stretched across his face. "No, no, I'm talking about when you asked me up to your place for coffee and I declined. I don't want you to think I'm the kind of guy who buys a few drinks and expects sex."

"Well, in this fantasy," I patted him on the chest, "I would have rocked your world."

"I'm sure you will."

Will? Dammit, he had this uncanny ability with a single word to send me reeling. From worried hero to seductive man, he'd prove a worthy adversary. My imagination moved into overdrive as it dissected his "will," until he was naked.

"Mr. Vex sent me to escort you upstairs. I thought it would be good to give you a quick briefing on the boss."

He led me to the elevator, giving a quick wave to the receptionist. As the doors opened, he placed a hand on the small of my back, guiding me inside. Each touch, no matter how innocent, I twisted into a sexual escapade.

"Damien can be rather intense. He has a clear vision for Revelations and is unwavering. As long as you pitch within that vision, he's open to feedback. He gives me plenty of slack to work with and allows us to be experts in what we do."

The small box working its way to the top of the building required us to stand in proximity. I wasn't sure if it was his shampoo, moisturizer, or cologne, but his scent had an intoxicating effect. Piano music filled the space, a random pop song made generic in an effort to ease the tension of being suspended hundreds of feet above certain death.

"That's refreshing." The Beacon had treated me like a grunt, a desk jockey who clicked the mouse in a mindless fashion.

"As a businessman, he's ruthless, and I can't emphasize that enough. He will go out of his way to destroy the competition." Did Sebastian think this was useful information, or was he attempting to give me a warning?

"Noted." Now the stress set in. If being jobless wasn't enough, now I had to fear setting off my one job prospect.

"With that being said, he has been nothing but supportive. He pushes us to be the best versions of ourselves. Be you. There's plenty to like. You'll win him over."

I was about to make a joke when Sebastian's pinky finger linked with mine. When I didn't pull away, he moved to intertwine our fingers. I had to resist the urge to push him against the wall and kiss him. At the same time, I didn't want to resist.

"Does this mean a second date is in order?" Chad would be proud of me. It was pretty much a certainty and lacked any risk as he squeezed my hand. There was something taboo about the touch. It took me a moment to remember I didn't work at the Beacon, and I wasn't dating the competition. Then it moved to dating a co-worker. Our dirty office romance would be the thing of legends.

"You're asking me out? Well, I'll have to check my calendar. I'm sure I could pencil you in."

I shot him a dirty look. There was something comfortable with the banter. If Sebastian had been all business, serious and straight faced, I wouldn't have been this smitten. His playfulness overlaid his serious demeanor, making him irresistible.

"Pencil me in." The elevator dinged as we reached our destination. "Maybe you'll get your world rocked."

His hand squeezed mine, but not in a gentle or cute

manner. Sexual frustration found its way into his grip, and I imagined that same hand reaching into my pants. I might be projecting, but just maybe, he was as worked up as me. There was a bit of satisfaction knowing he'd be thinking about my offer while at work. There's nothing sexier than a man in a suit, except a man in a suit with an erection.

"First," the doors opened, "let's see if you survive your interview."

Well, that killed my hard on.

Mr. Bossman's office had a classic look, similar to what you mind find in an old study, whereas Mr. Vex's office would be the antithesis. His office was lined with modern black shelves holding awards and trinkets, a display of his self-proclaimed greatness. His desk occupied the center of the room, a large piece of glass supported on a metal frame. Modern, minimal, expensive.

As I walked into the office, he was reviewing something on a tablet. With a single finger held up, telling me to wait, I had a chance to inspect the awards. Outstanding Businessman. Upcoming Entrepreneur. Faces to Watch. Industry Disrupter. Each of the glass sculptures spoke to his success as a businessman. Mr. Bossman had similar awards, but those spoke about the success of the magazine and less about personal accolades.

"Alright then," Damien set the table down and leaned back in his chair. The windows behind him were tinted, but with the sun high in the sky, it created a dark silhouette of the man. With the layout of the room and the carefully placed awards, it must be an intentional decision, all to add to the man's image.

"Thank you for seeing me so quickly," I managed.

I moved to one of the chairs opposite of his desk. The black leather was surprisingly comfortable. I could imagine after a long day of work, sitting in his office and drinking a celebratory whisky.

"Mr. Taylor spoke highly of you. He said that your work pushed boundaries at the Beacon." He crossed his legs. As he put his hands together, pointer fingers touching the sharp angle of his chin, he appeared like a classic Bond villain.

"I brought my portfolio for—"

"I'll take Mr. Taylor's word for it. I'm not sure how things are run at the Beacon, but I employ people I trust to run my business. I'm not a creative, and I won't step on the toes of people in that role."

I let out a sigh of relief. "That's a refreshing take."

"Let's get the formalities out of the way." He leaned forward, sliding the tablet out of the way as he rested his elbows on the glass. "Why did you decide to meet with Mr. Taylor?"

Did mentioning the man's sex appeal lack professionalism? I decided to go with a more business approach. "The climate at the Beacon has management in an adversarial position with the creative teams."

It was the best way to explain they were being assholes. Damien's face, cast in shadows, was incredibly difficult to read. I couldn't tell if he liked my answer or if he was mentally labeling me a troublemaker.

"What is the real reason?" He hardly moved as he pushed me against a wall. "The work climate isn't why you contacted Mr. Taylor."

Did he want to know about his employees dating? I had heard some bosses took liberties in what they considered professional, but that seemed out of character for a man who focused on his growing his business.

"I gave them an ultimatum and got fired."

"A man who stands up for his beliefs." Did Sebastian learn how to be cryptic from this man? Their inability to give contextual clues was alarming. I swore I'd never sit opposite of this man at a poker table.

"The Beacon." he stood slowly, exerting a mastery of core strength. He fastened the button on his blazer in a well-rehearsed motion, as if he were putting on body armor to prepare for battle. "It's a small-time operation that focuses on the wholesome aspect of superheroes. It's cute really, and you know what they say about cute?"

Was I supposed to answer? Cute is for kittens? Cute is

what my mother called me? Better to keep my mouth shut and let the man answer for himself.

"Cute doesn't sell. The Beacon has a diminishing readership, meanwhile the exposes of Revelations have seen a surge. People don't care about the Illuminator's favorite brownie recipe. They amount to puff pieces that lack any substance. Do you know what readers are really after?"

"Depth? The hidden lives of heroes?"

"Hidden," he chuckled at the statement. "Why do they hide behind masks? If they were noble, they wouldn't be hiding. The readers want to know who it is rescuing them. Not the media blitz put out by the Centurion's public relations team, but the *real* person behind the mask."

There had been numerous attempts to reveal the identities of superheroes. Only a few months ago, a reporter leaked the identity of Ultra. The footage had gone viral and within hours, villains discovered her very human husband. They used him as bait to lure her into a trap. While she survived, he hadn't. Since then, she and her daughter had gone into hiding. There were reasons, valid reasons, why heroes hid their identities from the public.

"I'm not saying they're all bad, or even that they have something to hide. But shouldn't we know if these vigilantes are convicts? Murderers? Law enforcement is powerless to stop them. The burden falls on the shoulders of the press."

Damien moved to the front of his desk, close enough to

invade my personal space. Leaning against the glass surface, my eyes were level with the buckle of his belt. For the first time in my life, I wasn't interested in speculating if the man wore boxers or briefs.

I cleared my throat. "But what can a publication do to stop a person capable of flying through the sun?"

Damien nodded his head, as if he were agreeing with me. While I desperately needed a job, I was kicking myself for not doing more than flipping through his magazine and studying the photography and layouts. Stupid me for not reading the articles and getting a sense of his slant on superheroes.

"These heroes believe they're untouchable, gods amongst men. Hell, some of them could withstand every weapon known to mankind. But thankfully, their vanity is their Achilles heel."

"Vanity, sir?"

"Without their worshippers, they're nothing. Why else would they be doing these necessary deeds? Every fist thrown, every bullet they deflect, it's so the public bows down to them. We have essentially transformed ourselves into their devoted servants. Revelations makes sure that their hubris doesn't go unchecked."

There were plenty of deniers in the public. Every day the news showed a small group of everyday people trying to convince Legislature to ban superheroes. Without them, we'd have been enslaved by alien races, underworld demons, or that guy always turning children's toys into weapons. As a planet, we were safer with them here, but I needed this job, so I kept my pro-hero point of view to myself.

"There should always be checks and balances," I said. I believed it, and with enough time, I'm sure Congress would develop some sort of system to collaborate with super-heroes, not work against them. Even now, the Centurions acted as governing body, ensuring that none of the top tier superheroes went unchecked.

"Griffin, we are that balance." He pushed off his desk and lazily walked around my chair. As he crossed out of my line of sight, the hair on the back of my neck stood on end. Something about this man didn't sit well with me, and it wasn't his volatile exchange with Bossman yesterday.

"Unlike the Beacon, I don't like the idea of designers working in isolation, nor the writers. If you're interested in a position, I'll want to see a full article package from you." His hand rested on my shoulder, and I feared anything but a resounding yes might result in him attempting to crush my collarbone.

I let out a nervous laugh at the thought. Spending so much time in a world of superheroes, my imagination ran away. Damien Vex might be a blow-hard, or even a terri-fying businessman, but that was it. The idea of such a high-profile man wearing a mask was borderline lunacy.

"A full package?" It was rare for designers to write articles, but on occasion we'd pitch in if the Beacon had been short staffed. If I didn't agree to this assignment, there was a good chance I wouldn't find another job. It wasn't as if Vincent or Bossman were going to write me a glowing recommendation after the ultimatum I gave them.

"Do you think you're up to the challenge, Mr. Smith?"

I took a moment to ponder the question. Did I think I was up to the challenge of writing, photographing, and designing a package for Revelations? I hadn't written a news article in over a year, so the thought of developing a piece worthy of Revelations terrified me. Could I be more than a lowly graphic designer? I couldn't handle another magazine destroying my confidence.

"Draft the article. If it has merit, and if it's worthy of space in Revelations, we'll assign a team to flesh it out. Unlike the Beacon, I believe in collaboration and part-nerships."

Sebastian Taylor.

My lip turned up as I recalled him talking about clawing his way out of poverty. As he described his successes, the pride he had in enjoying the finer things in life had been well earned. I might not be comfortable with his level of success, but perhaps it was because I had never tasted it before? If I could get my foot in the door at Revela-tions and make a name for myself as he had done, then perhaps it would leak it into other areas of my life.

I turned, losing count of the awards on shelves, back-lit

to make them stand out. He stepped away, framed by the numerous accomplishments. Somewhere deep inside, I wanted a taste. The desire to be more than a junior designer, a lowly nobody unable to get a seat at the table.

"Mr. Vex," I stood, holding out my hand, "you have yourself a deal."

His grin was almost as devilish as his frown. I shook his hand, the strength firm, but not overbearing. He wanted me to know he was fit, and more so, that he was calculated.

"This isn't a done deal. This is your interview, Mr. Smith. Don't disappoint." He let go of my hand and returned to his chair. Unfastening his jacket, he took his seat, hands crossed, pointer fingers pressed together.

"I'll have Mr. Taylor contact you in the next twenty-four hours to deliver our style guide. Say goodbye to the Beacon. You're about to become the person you were destined to be."

And with that, our meeting was over.

9

———

"I thought he was going to break me in half!"

"You should be so lucky to get tossed around like that." I glared at the cell phone. Obviously, Xander knew me too well. "You know I can see you giving me a death glare?"

"Seriously, he's scary. Not in a creep out from under the bed kind of way, but have you ever met somebody so confident that you wanted to run away?"

Xander screamed obscenities at somebody cutting off his ambulance. I had no idea where in the city he was driving, but like usual, the man's anger came across loud and clear. Eventually, we were going to need to have an intervention and suggest he take up yoga. He screamed again. Nope, skip yoga. Xander needed Xanax.

"Have we met?" Xander quipped. I should have known he wasn't the person to discuss insecurities. "Be careful of the guy. It sounds like he's an arrogant prick. You the know the kind. They talk a big game and flash their money, but the moment they drop their pants you understand why they try so hard."

"Perhaps. But I have a feeling this guy has money, and he's hung like a horse."

"Don't salivate."

I leaned back in my chair, eyeing the painting. It wasn't anything to hang in a gallery, but I was quite impressed with how it was turning out. It had been difficult to get the suit to look as if it were burning away from the hero, leaving his burly chest exposed. While the cowl hid the person's identity, it was painfully obvious that I had been remembering Sebastian as I painted it.

"You still there?"

"Sorry," I dropped my brushes into a cup of water. "I was painting when you called."

"Good," he said. "I'm glad to hear you're getting back into it. I've seen the painting you did for Bernard. I expected you to be more the type of guy who drew super-heroes." Xander didn't hide the annoyance in his voice every time he mentioned the people that caused him to work harder than normal.

"It's a superhero, isn't it?" he asked.

I laughed. "We need to stop hanging out so much. And yes, it's of a pretty hot superhero."

"Superhero porn, glad to know there's somebody out

there making it." Someday I would get to the root of his dislike for the capes protecting the city. Unfortunately, not tonight. "I have to go," he spat. "Wraith is at it again."

He hung up without explanation, a common occurrence when talking to him on the job. He must be pulling a twenty-four-hour shift if he was still out saving the city. It was ironic that for all his anger toward people with powers, he was a capeless hero.

I pushed the chair back, rolling along the living room. With a few feet between myself and the painting, I had to admit it wasn't half bad. The hair on his chest needed a bit more refining, and the shadow by his abs could be contoured further, but overall, it looked as if my hero had endured the worst a villain had to offer and stood proud, ready to protect the city.

And it didn't hurt that it looked like Sebastian. I had seen him without a shirt, but without decent lighting, I wasn't sure if his abs were this well-defined? I knew he had plenty of chest hair, but did it taper into a fine line that pointed to the promised land in his pants? Maybe someday I'd—

Knock. Knock. Knock.

I stared at my hands covered in paint. Apparently, being neat wasn't part of my process, and it was impossible to tell how I managed to get this dirty. The knock came at the door again, and I couldn't imagine who would be at my door this late in the evening.

"I'm coming, give me a second."

There was no point in being classy as I tried to wipe the paint on the front of my shirt. Pulling it off, careful to not leave streaks across my face, I flip it inside out, using the clean side to slide the chain from the lock.

"Excuse my appearance..."

With the door only half open, I debated throwing it shut and hiding. While I was covered in acrylics, looking like I lost a fight with a painting, Sebastian looked as dashing as ever. In school, they always speak about fight or flight, but they seldom include freeze. I couldn't move, not to run away and certainly not to hurl myself at the man.

"Did I catch you in the middle of something? I should have called. Stupid, I know. But Vex mentioned I needed to give you the magazine's style guide. It can wait until morning."

"Oh." Business. That made more sense as to why he was knocking at my door. I put aside my admiration and lust and focused on the job. I stared, trying to wrap my head around it when manners pushed their way through my libido. "Come in, come in. Sorry, my brain is in another place."

"You sure?" He didn't seem convinced.

"I was painting. When I'm in the zone, I forget the rest of the world exists." Okay, maybe that's not the entire truth, but it sure beat confessing to my awkwardness around him.

"Comic books and painting?"

My eyes dropped, eyeballing the paint covering my hands. The streaks of white I had used for the uniform had splattered across my fingers. I felt exposed, like I was standing in my birthday suit, and he was inspecting me. His words were neutral, but I knew the judgement. It had been a constant in my relationship with Dan. It was a foolish—

"I have a landscape painting hanging in my office. I couldn't tell you anything about the artist. It's a small cabin in the woods, away from the world. There's a light on in the cabin, which is weird, because there's no path leading to the porch. It's like the man living inside hadn't left in years. Sometimes when work gets stressful, I imagine I'm in there. My only job in the world is to make sure the fire never goes out. It's silly, I know."

"Not at all." I wanted to reach out and touch him, to put my hand on his cheek and see the fire in his eyes. Without realizing it, I had nearly placed my hand on his chest, stopping just before I soiled his suit.

With a slight shuffle, his chest touched my hand. Just like that, he ruined a perfectly good suit. When I tried to pull away, he stopped me, his hand pressing against mine. Through the suit, I could feel his heart thumping against his ribcage, his entire body vibrating in a quick steady rhythm.

"Our goodbye got ruined."

"An eventful first date."

"Sorry I didn't stay."

I gulped. "You're safe."

Our voices grew steadily quieter, as if somebody in the hallway might be listening to our conversation.

"Safe?"

"Your secret. It's safe with me." I meant it. Not only did I owe him for saving my life, but I owed him for outing himself and putting his identity in jeopardy.

"I *feel* safe." An admission. It wasn't a coy statement, beating around the bush. This confident man had not only revealed his biggest secret, but with it came the knowledge that he feared others knowing.

Out of habit, as he took another step closer, I backed up. With his foot, he slammed the door shut, cringing at the loud bang. While he stood in the doorway, our game of cat and mouse had remained innocent, but here, behind closed doors... There was nothing innocent about the look in his eyes.

I held my breath as he leaned forward, closing the gap between our faces. I closed my eyes, preparing for his lips to meet mine. I imagined the scruff of his beard tickling the soft gap of skin above my lip.

I waited until I finally had to exhale. Cracking my eyes, I could see he had moved onto something more exciting. Over my shoulder, I followed his eyes, trying to imagine what in my apartment was more thrilling than a half-dressed man.

"Oh."

Sebastian stepped past me, my hand pulled from his chest, leaving tiny specks of white paint. I was already embarrassed that this sexy man had caught me out of my clothes, but now he was seeing an infatuation being played out on a canvas. My head dropped, preparing for the mockery. At best, he tried to downplay it as he dropped off the style guide and vanished. At worst... well, there wasn't much worse than this.

"It's not a cabin in the woods," he said. "Wow. I don't know what to say."

"Don't say anything."

No indecision. No hesitation. No reluctance. He dropped the style guide as his hands moved to my neck, his thumbs pressed into my cheek. His lips tasted like cinnamon, as if he had been chewing gum from the corner store. Eager, he pushed hard enough that I worried he'd chip a tooth, but I'd risk it to make the taste of cinnamon permanent.

He broke the kiss. I leaned forward, chasing his lips, but they were pulled tight, smiling. Infectious, the devilish grin contaminated the air between us until I fell victim to the disease.

"I should go."

It was now or never.

"No," I whispered, "you shouldn't." Our admissions

became a two-way street, and I only prayed we travelled toward the same destination.

In place of words, he held up his left hand, fingers stretched as if he were willing them to grow. For a second, I wondered if he took advantage of them by playing the piano or guitar? His skin radiated a soft white light, barely visible despite squinting. It grew until the lines of his fingers vanished in a pool of white.

My hero was going nowhere.

As the steam poured off my skin, I inspected for any flecks of white I might have missed. I had forgotten how much of a wreck I had appeared in college. Once I was satisfied the evidence had washed down the drain, I stepped out of the shower and dried off in record time.

After a quick inspection in the mirror, I wrapped the towel around my waist and stepped into an empty living room. I had only been in the bathroom for a few minutes. Had Sebastian reconsidered the decision to stay?

I pushed away the negativity, and the world rewarded me. A trail of clothes started with his jacket. Then his dress shirt and last his slacks. Somewhere in the darkness of the bedroom, a man in nothing but underwear and dress socks awaited me. Imagining him sprawled out on my bed pushed aside the worry.

Stepping around his clothes, I stood in the doorway to the darkened bedroom. I reached for the light switch, wanting to see this gorgeous bear of a man waiting for me to crawl on top of him.

"Leave them off."

Okay, fine. Some people weren't comfortable with themselves naked. I could respect that. I could focus my—

"Let there be light," the words were soft, almost as much as the light emanating from the two dozen orbs hanging near the ceiling. The one closest to my head had an orange glow, just bright enough to make Sebastian visible.

"How are you doing this?"

"It's hard to explain. I do stuff with light."

I had a thousand questions, but as I focused on this man in his underwear leaning back in the bed, they didn't seem all that important.

He held up his hand in the universal sign of a gun and dropped his thumb. The shot fired, a crisp bit of yellow light striking my towel where it folded in on itself. The precision hit caused the terrycloth fabric to fall away, leaving me entirely exposed.

"Not your first time, I see," I said, raising my eyebrow.

He leaned forward on the bed, crossing his legs. "You're the first person to know about this." He pointed to the ceiling, several of the orbs shifting to a dark red. I couldn't decide what was more beautiful, the light show or the man in my bed. The orbs reacted, the light dimming until the entire room bathed in shades of red. It was a tie. His near-naked body under the lights was everything I could have asked for.

I ignored the fact I stood naked, package waving in the wind. "Are they dangerous?"

"These? No, not really."

"I meant your powers."

Sebastian hesitated. I opted for an easier question. "How did you get them?"

"I couldn't tell you. A year ago, I woke up in the middle of the night thinking it was daytime. My body was glowing like a nightlight."

"Have you—"

"Not to change the subject, but hate to let a naked guy go to waste."

Good point. I needed to push aside my obsession with superheroes so I could pay more attention to this sexy man. And with the way the red light covered his torso, I couldn't help but admire his fuzzy chest and how it tapered toward his navel, creating an arrow pointing at his crotch.

"I've got somebody's attention."

My erection betrayed me. There was no playing coy or witty banter. Climbing onto the bed, I worked my way over his body, pausing long enough to admire the outline of his cock. Boxer briefs, good choice. I dipped low, kissing his chest. I wanted to drag out the admiration, to put my lips on every part of his body, but Sebastian proved to be impatient. Grabbing under my arms, he pulled me up his body.

He kissed as if it might be his last. Eager. Passionate. The stubble along his upper lip scratched my face, reminding me that I had this masculine hunk of a man under me, his hands roaming up the center of my back. As I pulled away to take a breath, he followed, biting my lower lip, holding me in place. I gasped as he teetered between pain and pleasure.

His smooth hands stopped massaging my back, and I thought we were prepared to move onto the next event. His fingertips grazed the space between my shoulder blades, delicately touching my skin as they traveled downward. I let out a gasp as each point of contact turned electric.

I lowered myself until I was resting my weight on his body, my face buried in his neck. A man might act as if his cock were the most sensual place to be touched, but it's a lie we tell the world. My erection softened, and yet I had never been this turned on. The heat of his hand gave away its location, and every time his fingers made gentle contact, I gasped, craving more.

"I could get used to this." He spoke the words softly, as if he were reading my mind. The electricity pooled at the base of my spine, traveling downward as he cupped my ass, giving it a firm squeeze.

"You can do that all you want." I hope he—

Sebastian rolled me over, putting me on my back in a

single graceful motion. His arms were muscular, but not so much that he should be able to toss me about with such ease. As he straddled my body, I realized that the orbs floating about the room might not be the only ability he possessed.

I was about to ask when he flicked his tongue across my nipple. It might not be the most erogenous part of my body, but the rough texture against my skin forced my back to arch. I moaned as his teeth replaced his tongue. I don't know how I got this lucky, but I didn't want him to stop.

He travelled down my body, scooting along until he hovered over my cock. It stood at attention, straight up in the air, begging for the same attention he showed the rest of my body. He leaned in close enough I could feel the warmth of his breath along the bottom of my shaft.

"Enjoying yourself?" The smirk gave away his teasing.

"Uh, huh." There was no point in pretending he was going to get coherent words from me. He took my hand, placing it on the back of his head, signaling that he wanted me to take control. As his lips circled the head of my cock, I fell victim to his impatience.

Pulling him down, the heat of his mouth covered my cock. I let my fingers pull at his hair, lifting him and dragging him down until it was buried in his mouth. With a buck of my hips, I could feel the bend of his throat, and like a champ, he managed to swallow the length of my hard on.

"Fuck," I gasped. I hated to admit it, but it had been a

while since I had a man in bed, especially one this eager. I lifted his head off my cock, fearful that the evening was about to reach its climax. I wanted to drag out the experience, to revel in Sebastian's expertise.

He slid down further, turning his attention to my sack. He managed to get both testicles in his mouth, careful to take his time. With a firm grip, he squeezed my cock, not stroking, just reaffirming that it was his to play with. I admired his confidence, each action executed with a precision that drove me wild. I wanted to repay the favor.

Hands slid under my legs, pushing them back, making it clear the direction the evening was going to take. There was a pause, a long enough space where somebody might protest the next step, but as I pulled my legs back, I let him know how badly I wanted him to continue.

I moaned as his tongue trailed down the space under my balls until he reached my ass. With a light stroke of my cock, I couldn't pick which to focus on. It wasn't about the way he drilled his tongue in and out, but about the next event. I liked Sebastian, but it wasn't as if I let any man fuck me. Did I trust that this wouldn't be a one-and-done?

He worked his way up my body, kissing my dick and then my stomach, resting my legs over his shoulders. Even through his underwear, I could feel his hardness and its determination to tear through the fabric. Amazed at my sex induced flexibility, he leaned in, stealing a kiss.

"What do you want?"

Just like when I guided his mouth down the length of my cock, he relinquished his power. This beautiful man, this downright *hot* bear of a man, let me decide my fate. As I pulled my legs back, grinding my ass against his groin, I decided to take the plunge. Or was that the other way around?

"You sure?"

Consent, who said it couldn't be sexy?

"I want you in me."

Snaking a hand behind my neck, he used that uncanny strength to lift me off the bed, pushing his lips against mine. He lacked his previous grace as he reached into his underwear, tucking it under his package. It wasn't the length that was impressive, it was the girth. Suddenly, I was grateful he had spent time rimming.

"Take it slow," I sighed.

"Always," he whispered, leaning in for another kiss.

He sat upright on his knees, spitting into his hand and coating the head of his massive cock. He guided it to my ass, forcing a gasp from my lips as he found his mark. It might be a challenge, but in that moment, I wanted nothing more than this man buried inside me.

He took his time, studying my face as he gave his hips a slight push. My entire body tensed at the sensation, pleasure rippling along my skin. He paused. With a deep breath, I relaxed, and when he didn't attempt more, I pushed myself down his shaft.

"Damn," he moaned. With one long and steady stroke, the entire length slid in. He turned his head, kissing along my calf, moaning in between. "I jerked off thinking about this moment."

Wait, he masturbated thinking about me?

He dipped low, wrapping an arm behind my back, lifting me off the bed as if I weighed nothing. My legs dropped from his shoulders, wrapping around his waist as he held me tight against his chest. I finally understood Alejandro's obsession with bedding superheroes.

"You are beautiful." The kiss came with a thrust, and I moaned at the feeling of him buried deep in me. It was near my limit, close enough that I had to relax as he held me in place, fucking me with long steady strokes.

"It feels amazing." I wrapped my arms around his neck, savoring the sensation of my cock grinding between our stomachs. The electric sensation returned, this time originating from my body. There was no point resisting. "I'm going to cum."

His hands moved to my ass, thrusting faster. He chased my orgasm, trying to cum at the same time. I reached the finish line first, my body trembling as I came without touching myself. It was a first, and as I coated our torsos, I hoped it wasn't the last.

"I'm going to cum." I could feel his cock swell, causing mine to shoot another volley. His skin glowed, a soft white radiating until it filled the room. It grew brighter as he shoved the length in me, letting out a low growl. He held still for a moment before giving me one last thrust. I thought I might faint, the endorphins pumping through my veins.

He kissed my neck while otherwise remaining frozen in place. It was the dreaded post-sex conundrum. Be sore or risk the overwhelming sensation on the withdraw. Thankfully, he pulled out, gasping as his cock slipped from my ass.

"Damn," he said between kissing.

"Damn, indeed."

He didn't make any indication he was going to set me down, instead giving me a quick kiss on the lips.

"Well, that was hot," he said.

I couldn't have anticipated my evenings ending quite like this.

"I'll make sure to leave high marks on your comment card."

"Shower?" He looked down, a tiny dribble of white near in the center of his chest. I nodded in reply, feeling absolutely no guilt that I had drenched the man.

"If my legs work." The cramps were ready to set in, the awkward position of my legs wrapped around him growing more difficult to maintain.

"I guess I'll have to carry you."

And he did.

10

"SPILL."

"I can see it in your eyes."

"I can smell the sex on you."

We hadn't been sitting at the table for sixty seconds when Bernard grew silent. Neither Alejandro nor Xander noticed at first, until the burly bear across the table narrowed his eyes and thrust a finger in my direction. The gig was up, and there was no way this breakfast ended without me confessing.

"Xander, thanks for noticing my eyes. And Alejandro," I took a bite of my bagel, "when don't you smell sex?"

"Deflecting!" Bernard barked. "If I have to reach across this table..."

"Whoa," I leaned back, fearful he might make good on his promise. "I might have had a date last night."

Alejandro leaned in, pretending to sniff the air. "He reeks of sin."

I wanted to hold a straight face and ignore their prodding. But when I thought back to the previous night, I'm certain my face betrayed me. Sebastian had tossed me over his shoulder and only set me down once we reached the shower. Two big men in a small space had been comical, and listening to his hissing every time he bumped against the cold tile had been endearing. As we toweled off, I dreaded the night ending, and when he slipped on his boxer briefs, I willed my way past the fear.

My face turned hot as I recalled uttering one simple word. Stay. I thought my heart would jump out of my chest as I waited for his response.

My hands turned sweaty as Bernard reached for the knife.

"Fine! His name is Sebastian, and yes, he spent the night."

Alejandro slapped Bernard's hand away from the knife, taking it himself. In an almost threatening manner, he waived it about.

"If you don't give us details, we fight!"

I recounted the night. I tried to skimp on details once I got out of the shower. All three of them peppered me with questions until I relented. I divulged every wet detail of the encounter. More than once, Xander sprung to his feet, apologizing as he adjusted himself. Even Alejandro reached for his phone, texting a booty call, saying he'd need to let off some steam after this.

I paused after I confessed to being scared, asking him to stay. If it were anybody else, I would have skipped the detail, but I wanted that internal nagging sensation out on the table.

"What if I really like this guy?"

A cup of coffee came out of nowhere, thrust onto the table by Chad. I hadn't seen the coffee shop's owner as I recounted my escapades.

"Dear God," he dropped into a crouch, eyes fixated on me. "What did he say?"

"He hadn't planned on leaving." The idea that the sexy man had made the decision to spend the night before I asked it made my heart ache. "Apparently he just sleeps in his underwear."

Xander and Alejandro started on a debate about men sleeping with clothes on. Bernard gave me a smile before confessing he wore briefs to bed. Part of me expected them to gush over the realization, perhaps even give me a pep talk. To an onlooker, it might have seemed they were being shallow, and maybe they were, but they didn't feel I needed motivation. It was subtle, but I sat up straighter at the thought.

Chad rested on a hand on my knee. "It couldn't have happened to a sweeter guy. I haven't seen you with that goofy smile in a long time." He took my half-finished coffee, leaving behind the fresh cup.

I took a sip as Xander tried to explain to Bernard why keeping his testicles bound while sleeping was a bad idea. When Alejandro commented on wanting easy access to any cock sleeping in his bed, I nearly spit out my coffee.

All eyes turned, threatening to bore holes through my head. Bernard cleared his throat. "Tricky, tricky, Griffin. You almost got away with it." He leaned back in his chair, arms folding across his chest. "There's more, isn't there? Spill it."

There was no point in hiding the smile, a grin stretching from ear-to-ear. For once, it wasn't Alejandro discussing a fling from the club, or Xander lamenting how he never had time to date. All attention was on me as I started with, "It was barely light out when Sebastian started kissing the back of my neck..."

"Where are we?"

"We're on the outskirts of the Ward. It's the one part of the city the gays haven't gotten their hands on. The only life you'll find out here is when there's a rave."

We had taken the subway to the end of the line and continued walking. Sebastian had managed to finish his work by noon, but not before texting me a photo of him in the bathroom with his pants around his ankles, pointing at the white stain I created this morning. He feigned complaining that next time he stayed the night he'd bring a change of underwear, so he didn't smell of sex while at work.

"I'm not sure you understand how a lunch date works. Usually there's food, maybe a cocktail. Hell, you could have convinced me for an afternoon roll in the sack, but empty warehouses? Isn't this where supervillains hide?"

He wasn't wrong about... wait, had he thought I texted him for a nooner? I made sure to put a mental pin in that conversation for tomorrow. We had dined at a fancy restaurant far out of my league. It was time he got to see the world through my eyes.

"You know I'm a comic book fan."

"I did notice the stack on the nightstand."

"And that I love superheroes."

"I remember the artwork."

I took him by the hand, dragging him past the broken door of a warehouse. I couldn't tell if it had been a car factory, or perhaps they created machine parts, but it was empty and large enough for afternoon shenanigans.

"Yeah, so..." I spun about, arms flung open wide. "You didn't want to talk about it last night. I didn't bring you here to talk. I wanted to see you in action. It's not like I know many superheroes."

Sebastian rolled his eyes. "How do you know I'm not the villain in this story?"

The man had a point, and if his suit wasn't wrinkled from spending the night on my floor, I might say he looked the part. The only missing element was the perfectly manicured mustache. If he hadn't risked exposing himself to save me from Wraith, perhaps I'd have been worried. But when he jeopardized his secret for me, he had cemented his status as a superhero.

"What villain plays with Legos? You're new to this. I can understand why you'd fear having powers. So, I'm here to be the faithful sidekick."

"I'm not scared. I just have no ambition to be one of those goons wearing capes flying around the city. I can think of better things to do with my time."

"You talk about a rough upbringing in Southlands, imagine the difference you could make there."

The mention of his childhood home garnered a less than thrilled expression. I made a mental note to be tread carefully when discussing the rough side of Vanguard.

"If you learned how to — "

He kicked a brick on the ground, launching it into the air. It sailed the length of the warehouse, smashing through a grungy window. Sebastian gestured in the comet's direction. "I have a handle on the powers."

"Humor me." I patted him on the chest before leaning over a cement slab almost waist height. "Then maybe I'll let you rail me again."

"Did you just bribe me with sex?"

"Is it working?"

He unfastened his jacket, tossing it on the slab. With a fast slap on the ass, he started rolling his sleeves. He loosened the tie and flexed his arms, showing off the muscles under his shirt. Even without the suit, his biceps bulged enough that I could imagine him filling out a leather suit and fighting crime.

"So, what exactly is your power?"

"You're the comic book fan. You should be telling me."

"So far, I've seen you glow, shoot a towel off me, and create some pretty amazing mood lighting. Since sexy isn't a power, I'll have to go with light, right?"

He nodded. Closing his eyes, he shook his shoulders, working it down into his hands. I held my breath, waiting for something to happen. He let out a sigh, adding a shoulder roll, and cracking his neck.

"I can't do it with you watching me."

"Well, you're going to need to get over that," I said. The frustration humanized him. For all the cockiness and confidence, it was endearing to see him struggle with something. Sebastian's lack of perfection made him even sexier.

"You seemed to do just fine yesterday."

"I wasn't exactly focused on showing off yesterday. I had a lot of other things to be nervous about."

"Nervous, you say?"

His skin flared, projecting light, as if a silent bomb went off. For the briefest of seconds, there was no warehouse, just an infinite white. It vanished quickly as it began, leaving orbs dancing in my vision. It seemed the moment he stopped thinking about his abilities, they were readily available. Mental note made.

"Well, that's," I rubbed my eyes, "*enlightening.*"

"Puns? Really? So, we're going to have that type of relationship."

My back straightened at the mention of the "R" word. If he was going to put it on the table, I'd have to give it some thought. Before I got flustered, I decided to move on to the next demonstration.

"Okay, so you have strength, and you're a human lightbulb. What about that shooting light thing? Can you do that on command?"

I searched around the floor until I found a discarded beer bottle. Placing it on the ledge, I stepped away. If he could knock the towel off me at ten paces, I was probably safe, but I didn't want to test it.

He held up his hand as if he were a kid playing cops and robbers. He steadied himself, staring down the length of his arm. Dropping his thumb like the hammer, a ray of white light shot from his hand, missing the bottle by a few inches.

"Okay, so hitting the towel was sheer luck?"

He growled, trying again. Missing the bottle a second and third time, he grumbled a string of curses. Making two fists, he banged his hands together and a blast of light, far bigger, shot from his knuckles, obliterating the bottle and a piece of the ledge underneath it.

"Okay, we're moving into the impressive category."

He rolled his eyes. "You know I'm not a superhero. The only way I'm dressing up in leather is if we go to the BDSM club."

"I... I... How do I respond to that?"

"You're cute when you get flustered."

Damn him. The frustrated hero vanished and in his place, stood the cocky art director. He might not think he was a superhero, but all the elements were there. He could be another person fighting against the corruption rampant in Vanguard. Sebastian might think money, or a flashy title, deemed him a Southland success story. But if he could turn around and be a hero to his younger self, then he could inspire an entire generation.

"What about the floating lights?"

His skin glowed for a moment, not as bright, but unlike before, he let the light travel down his arm. Pooling in the palm of his hand, an orb appeared. With a gentle nudge, it lifted into the air and remained suspended as if by magic.

"And you can control them?"

Poking the sphere with his finger, it glided the twenty feet between us, stopping inches from my face. He walked closer as the orb shifted from white to blue to red. I reached out, touching it with the tip of my finger. It had a weight to it, like a dense bubble.

"It's not exactly super material like this." He plucked it from the air and chucked into the warehouse. Without a sound, it exploded, blowing the dust along the floor.

"So last night, my apartment was filled with explosive lights? You filled my bedroom with bombs!"

He raised an eyebrow, thinking about it for a moment. "I guess I wasn't thinking with the head on my shoulders."

"Don't get me wrong, it was sweet, just try not to kill me."

"Have to save something for the next date."

Chad had a list of rules he always spouted to the love-struck. Amongst them was, "Plan the next date before the current date is over." I had laughed at the forwardness of the advice, but it seemed I had missed this lesson in Dating 101. Apparently, I was the only person to not get this memo.

"I'm going to go out on a limb, and don't kill me." He didn't like mentioning his upbringing, but I couldn't let it go. "Imagine the children of Southland having their very own hero."

"I don't—"

"Imagine if you had that hero growing up? Somebody who got out, made a name for themselves and came back to speak for those who got trapped?"

"I'm not a hero."

He started to unroll his sleeves. I had never met a man so defensive about the location he once called home. It was dangerous territory, and I knew I risked creating a wedge in whatever *this* was between us. For me, it had been comic books that gave me a glimpse into a better world. But the people in those pages were real. They walked amongst us. That was what the world needed.

"You're already a hero. Giving money to your high school? That's what heroes do. Now you have something more than money. You are literally a shining beacon."

"I..." He paused, one sleeve unrolled and fastened. His shoulders slumped as his eyes darted back and forth. I couldn't imagine what he had to deal with growing up in the roughest part of Vanguard City, but I knew pain when I saw it. Time to be the hero Sebastian needed.

I walked up to him while his mind was elsewhere. Putting my arms around his neck, he came to, eyes focused on my face. I leaned in, kissing him. It started tentatively, and slowly his body loosened, melding against mind until his hand reached between my shoulder blades and pulled me closer.

"You saved me the other night. You're already a hero."

I rested my forehead against his, savoring the embrace.

"No suit," he grumbled.

I smiled. "I prefer you out of the suit."

His laugh broke the tension. "What do the heroes in your comics do now?"

"This is where we'd begin a training montage."

In Vanguard City, we had grown accustomed to the dangers of supervillains hurling cars or overlords from a parallel dimension threatening to enslave us. We accepted this strange reality. But it didn't mean I wanted to send Sebastian into the world without knowing he was capable. What kind of sidekick would that make me?

He stepped back, pulling his tie over his head and handing it to me. He unbuttoned his dress shirt and tossed it over my shoulder. Sebastian had sex appeal all on his own, but when he pulled the undershirt from his pants, peeling it off, I let out a low whistle.

"Okay, let's do this."

When this was over, the only thing he'd being *doing* was me.

11

———————

"Xander is the one with a sex addiction?"

"That's Alejandro. Xander is the one with anger management issues."

"And Bernard is the daddy bear?"

I had to pause and think about it. He was older than me by at least a decade, but I'm not sure I ever thought of him hitting "daddy bear" status. "I'm going to say yes. But if he finds out, I'll deny it."

For the last hour, we wandered around Vanguard's Institute of Modern Art. I didn't want to congratulate myself, but this was a good idea for a date night. There were as many differences between us as there were similarities. For two people in the business of making things look beautiful, this a perfect way to refill the creative well.

"So what exactly is this brunch thing you guys do?"

"We get together every day to start the day. It's just a way to catch up. Sometimes we gossip, sometimes we complain about men—"

"Have I come up?"

Sneaky, Sebastian. He caught me in my own trap. If I lied now, I'd appear uninterested. If I admitted to talking about him, I'd embarrass myself.

"Your cheeks answered that one." He patted me on the face. This is why I never played poker. My face gave away every thought.

"I might have mentioned you. You know, in a casual passing kind of way." Okay, that was a lie. I had downright bragged about this sexy man who I continued catching staring at me when he thought I wasn't looking.

"I look forward to meeting them."

The white hallway gave way to a large room with a single installation. While many of the pieces in the museum cycled in and out of fashion, this had been a mainstay since they moved to this location. Suspended from the ceiling were strands of fishing line holding burnt embers, remnants of the artist's childhood home.

"What do we have here?" Sebastian leaned in close to one of the lines, inspecting the burned wood. It appeared as if it were a fire frozen in time.

"She watched as her home burned down. Once the fire was put out, she collected the pieces in some attempt to hold onto her identity. Something about it always hits me right in the feels."

"Destructive and beautiful."

While the strands suspended from the ceiling, holding hundreds of pieces of wood, they weren't anchored to the floor. Sucking in a deep breath, I forced the air from my lungs. The embers moved back and forth, mirroring the effects of a massive fire sending smoke into the air.

Sebastian didn't speak. I studied his face as he stepped back from the installation. It had been nearly a year since attending the museum, and even longer since I brought company. Dan had never appreciated art, and found it overly complicated or so simple he believed he could have made it.

"That's," Sebastian let out a long sigh, "intense."

I had traded up. As he gave his head a slight shake, I wanted to pounce. If I pinned him to the corner, the patrons walking by might believe the two guys furiously going at it might be a work of art exposing carnal pleasures. I wasn't one for public sex, but I'd gladly make an exception for Sebastian.

The wandering continued.

The next room was the largest in the gallery. Easily the side of a basketball gallery, paintings taller than me were sparsely hanged, giving each of them breathing room. In the middle, a fake wall divided the space, not quite reaching the ceiling. It held a graffiti style mural that must have measured fifty feet wide by twenty tall. There was no way to avoid the immensity of the work.

"Did you plan this?"

It took a moment before I realized the figures portrayed with spray paint were superheroes. Moving from left to right, it showed the progression of a man cowering in fear on the street to a hero with his cape waving in the wind while he prevented a building from collapsing. Having read comics for most of my life, I recognized an origin story when I saw one. I didn't recognize the suit, but the theme, mundane to super, that was familiar.

"I swear, I had no idea." We had spent the last several days at the warehouse, running through the list of potential powers at his disposal. He was content to practice, but every time I mentioned donning a suit and protecting the city, he balked at the idea.

"It reminds me of the street art I discovered in Berlin."

"Berlin?" I should have guessed that somebody like Sebastian had travelled the globe. While he took the company jet for destinations unknown, I could count the states I had visited on one hand.

"I found the artist and managed to commission him to do a few pieces for me." He didn't flaunt his money, but it was obvious that we came from two different worlds. I didn't mind the finer things in life, it was my paycheck that did. But with the new job at Revelations, a senior level position would finally allow me to stop counting pennies.

"I still don't understand the infatuation. Why does having powers require being a hero?"

Okay, our difference in lifestyle, that I could overlook. But his inability to see how the power at his disposal could change the world, that required a certain level of being tone deaf.

"If a villain murders a thousand people, and you have the ability to stop it, shouldn't you?"

"I didn't ask for that responsibility."

"Nobody asks to be a hero. It's what you do." He fixated on the painting, studying it the same way he had the burned embers. "It's *right* thing to do."

"I'm not saying it's off the table. But if it happens, it's my choice. I don't owe anybody anything. I'm sure there's more like me. We're just trying to get by in life."

"If those people all stood up," I eyed the gigantic superhero stoping the building from crushing a young child. "Then the world would be a better place."

There were plenty of sidekicks who put on leather and followed their hero into battle. In comics almost every hero had their companion, a smaller version of themselves. But it was the ones who provided a moral compass for the hero that made for the most compelling stories. I couldn't fight, and unless I found Neptune's trident, I had no powers to speak of. But as I turned to inspect Sebastian's face, I understood my role.

"You're not going to let this go, are you?"

I had to believe there was a hero somewhere inside Sebastian. I don't think I could hear about the injustice in the world and let him standby. At the same time, I didn't want it to create a wedge between us this early in dating.

"Have you ever gone axe throwing?" We could finish this conversation for another time. Right now, I wanted to laugh with Sebastian and get to know him as a man. We'd deal with his superhero persona later.

"What is axe throwing?"

"It's awesome. You drink cheap beer and throw axes."

"This seems dangerous."

"It certainly is," I smiled. "That's what makes it fun."

I took the man by the hand, leading him toward the exit. He might lead a life of luxury, but I questioned if he ever had fun. Okay, so I had two goals as a sidekick, turn into into a hero and teach him to stop and enjoy life.

"Wait until they bring out the blindfolds. Then you'll get to see my skills."

He chuckled at my bravado. "Supervillains aren't looking all that dangerous right now."

12

———

"What about Shimmer?"

"No."

"Human Lightbulb?"

"It's like you're not even trying now."

We cleared the exit of the subway terminal, somewhere near the financial district of Vanguard City. After a day of training, we decided it was time to return to the mundane life. At first, I thought he meant to end our date, but when he suggested a shower at his place, I eagerly accepted.

"You'd think after years of reading comic books I'd be better at this. It's like all the good names are taken."

"I know you're excited about whatever this is," he held up his hand, flexing his fingers. "But I'm not a hero. I'm a poor kid from Southland, we're not bred to be heroes. Survivors, maybe, but definitely not heroes."

Without any fanfare, he reached out, hooking his pinky around mine. We had spent a night together. Hell, I held this massive secret of his, but this was weirdly intimate. The grand gestures might make a statement, but the little ones, they're what led me to believe this might be a long-term arrangement. Now, if only I could convince him to embrace the hero buried within.

"Switching topics." I'd revisit his reasons to not gift the world with his abilities. "Based on what I know about you, the bed will be perfectly made."

"I hope so, or I'm paying the maid too much."

"Maid? Really?"

I didn't want to judge, especially since he hadn't made any indication that there was an income chasm between us. Instead, I judged myself, embarrassed for not getting my act together sooner and switching to a new company.

"Once we're done with that shower, you can help me prep work for Damien." I give him a big smile, so he knew what I had planned.

He rattled off a list of things Damien loved and loathed, and I tried to keep a mental ledger. Thankfully, the vibration in my pocket interrupted his tirade about page number placement.

"It's the HeroApp™, isn't it?"

"I'm making a bet that somebody is stealing cats and putting them in trees." I reached for the phone.

"Not around here. We're in the heart of the city. Plenty

of hostages and death. A few weeks ago, somebody blew up a building and Timex had to go back in time to stop it."

He wasn't wrong, but I still let out a long sigh when I found out it was Wraith. Cobalt and Zipper had already responded to the call and were in progress of defeating her. Their icons were less than a block away and before I could comment, black X's crossed out the heroes' names.

"She defeated Zipper and Cobalt." It was hard to believe that within the span of seconds, she had beaten the two veteran heroes from the Ward.

Sebastian looked over my shoulder at my phone. "Wait, a second," he said, plucking the phone from my hand. "That's my block. I'm two buildings down."

"Do we wait?" I'll admit, I didn't want to. I was standing next to a hero in the making. He might not be ready to take on Wraith, but on-the-job training would be better than shooting cans in an abandoned warehouse.

"I think we can sneak in on the other side of the street."

Okay, not exactly the rush in and save the day attitude I hoped for, but I'd take it. Part of me was jealous, wishing I had some flashy supernatural ability so I could swoop in. Afterward, I'd be sipping gin with Zipper and Cobalt, as I recounted how I saved the day. If only Sebastian shared my penchant for heroics.

"If you think it's safe." I tried to hide my excitement.

If we got close enough to the action, then Sebastian could jump in and reveal his uncanny abilities. He'd be catalogued in the HeroApp™ and in no time, he'd be considered ranked amongst the greats.

"Wipe that grin off your face. We're not going to have some epic showdown."

"I didn't — "

"You're definitely thinking it."

"I would never." I was such a bad liar.

He didn't move a muscle except for the narrowing of his eyes. With a simple gesture, he went from handsome to downright sinister. I hardly knew him, and already he was reading my mind. Wait, was that one of his superpowers, or was I just that damned transparent?

"Fine." Yes, I pushed my lip out to pout.

"I can either save the day," he grabbed me by the loop of my jeans and pulled me close, "or I can fuck you in the shower."

Okay, he made my decision a bit more complicated. I wanted to ask if both were an option, but he kissed me, burying his tongue in my mouth.

"You're lucky my cock is doing the thinking right now," I panted.

He leaned in close, his cheek pressed against mine.

"Me?" His voice quieted to a breathy whisper. "Maybe I'll drop the soap and you'll be the lucky one."

My pants tightened.

"Help, she's going to kill me!"

The sphere of black gave away Wraith's terrorizing of the building across the street. Her abilities had covered the entrance to the sky rise lobby. The darkness spread into the street, half consuming a collection of empty cars with opened doors. The drivers had fled, abandoning their vehicles to make sure they weren't victims.

Sebastian had made it clear he didn't want to get involved, and I had reluctantly agreed. I couldn't push him into heroing if he wasn't ready for it. But as a man's high-pitched voice filled the street, I froze.

"I know that voice."

"What?" Sebastian gave my arm a tug, trying to get me into the revolving door leading into his lobby. The thought of Sebastian naked and covered in soap should have been a priority, but—

"She's going to kill me!" The voice came from somewhere in the darkness. Shriller than usual, I almost didn't put a face to the scream.

"It's Vincent."

"Your old boss? Good riddance. Let Wraith do what she wants with him."

I ignored the cold words. Vincent deserved a swift kick to the groin, but he didn't deserve death. With Cobalt and Zipper out of the mix, who knew how long it'd be before one of the big names in the superhero world came to the rescue. If only I could get Sebastian to jump in there. He might not be capable of defeating her, or even getting her locked up, but a minor victory could be what he needed to turn him into a full-fledged superhero. He did it once in the alley, but that had been for...

I pulled my arm free and ran across the street. Vincent's screams broke through the sphere of darkness. It was stupid, but if it took putting myself in danger to get a reaction from Sebastian, I'd have to do it. I might not rescue Vincent, but I could force Sebastian's hand.

I dashed into the darkness. It was like I had closed my eyes in the middle of the night or been buried alive. Without an ounce of light penetrating her aura of evil, I feared I'd suffocate. But her abilities had no substance, just the absence of light. Thankfully, Vincent continued screaming like a b-rate horror movie, and I moved my way toward him.

Somewhere inside this cloud, Wraith waited. I tried not to think about her, but as I bumped into something, I yelped. Waist high, the object was harder than a human, and with a quick inspection I realized I almost peed myself over a fire hydrant. Maybe this wasn't a smart idea.

What if Sebastian didn't come to the rescue?

Vincent wailed again. It dawned on me that there were no other voices. Had Wraith released the other people wandering the street to focus on Vincent? He was an arrogant jerk and probably had a wad of cash in his pocket, but not enough to risk going to jail.

Something shoved me from behind with enough force that it sent me flying. I screamed before landed with a thud, rolling until I bumped into a quivering mass. Vincent yelped as I grabbed his pants, trying to pull myself upright.

"I know you." Wraith's voice didn't originate from any specific direction. It echoed in the darkness, an ominous smooth hiss that fitted her superpowers.

"Leave him alone," I shouted.

"No." She responded with a coy voice, playful, as if she considered this a game.

"Stop her!" Vincent screamed.

Come on, Sebastian.

"I won't let you kill him."

"Your efforts are amusing." I wanted to punch into the darkness and pray that my knuckles connected with the villain.

Something snaked around my leg, pulling me away from Vincent.

"Stop!"

"I was only going to kill this pathetic human, but I can make room in my schedule for two murders."

In the distance, a single pinpoint of light broke through her walls of black. The thing clawing at my leg let go as the light spread. Whatever violated her domain required her attention. A light flooded the darkness, forcing me to shield my eyes.

"Who dares—"

Wraith screamed.

Sebastian. Except, instead of a hunky man, he was nothing more than a human shaped lightbulb. It was ironic that a woman capable of manipulating shadows was about to get thumped by her polar opposite. He shone brightly enough that I couldn't do more than glance in his direction before my eyes narrowed to slits.

I had gambled with my life to ensure Sebastian became the hero I knew he could be. What was death compared to helping destiny along? I never thought I could save Vincent, but I could give Sebastian incentive. Now I prayed he fulfilled his end of my plan.

"Leave him alone."

"Or what?" Wraith hissed.

"Try me." His voice was deeper, richer, as if he had practiced this voice a thousand times before. It wasn't far off from his bedroom voice. I batted away the thought of the hero naked in bed.

Accepting his challenge, she lifted from the ground and sped toward him. It happened quickly. The tearing of the car door, hurling it at Wraith. Her tendrils of darkness caught it and heaved it to the side. I don't know if it was intentional, but the door now sped toward me and Vincent. At the last moment, a blast of light struck the shard of metal. Redirecting the projectile, Sebastian sent it smashing through the window of Vincent's building.

It was black and white fists pummeling the other. Every

time the claws of her shadows clutched his limbs, he flared a bright white until they retreated. I crawled to my knees when a blast of light hammered against Wraith. She landed only a few feet away, a human arm exposed from the liquid black.

"He's winning," I whispered.

The darkness crept down her arm until she returned to a living shadow. She jumped to her feet and raised her hand in the air as it transformed into a long, slender blade. I guess if she couldn't stop Sebastian, she'd settle on impaling me and Vincent.

"Don't let her kill me," Vincent whined.

He shoved me forward, using me as a human shield. Did he realize it was a former employee trying to save him, or did he not care who died? I knew he was a snake, but—

Wraith brought her arm down. I clenched my eyes, waiting. A second passed before I stole a peek, certain she was dragging out my agony. A steady stream of light from Sebastian's chest pummeled her, pushing her out of striking distance. The shadows she wore like armor peeled back, revealing human flesh underneath.

"Kill her!" Vincent yelled. I turned and shoved the man, returning the favor. He tripped over his feet, landing on his tailbone with a sharp hiss.

The light show vanished with Wraith on her knees, struggling to maintain her cloak of shadows. Sebastian had nearly turned her, but the black clung to her face and continued down the left side of her body. Her chest was exposed, natural and human. Hanging between her breasts was a green pendant, the only article of clothing the supervillain appeared to be wearing.

"This isn't over!" she screamed.

She shot straight up, soaring alongside the high-rise. By the time she reached the top, I turned my attention to Sebastian, or I would have. In true superhero fashion, he had blinked out of sight, vanishing into thin air.

"A lot of good you did," Vincent spat.

"You've got to be kidding me." I spun around, fingers drawn tight, prepared to slug the man. While he was wailing like a damsel in distress, I had nearly gotten myself cleaved in half. He'd been more than willing to let me die so he could get one more scream in.

I froze. It started in my gut, a rumble that quickly grew until I was lost in a belly laugh. The sight of Vincent, a man who considered himself untouchable, drenched in his own piss, was exactly the gift from Heaven I needed.

He glanced down, cursing as I continued pointing and laughing. I walked away, crossing the street as citizens returned to their vehicles. One man stood at his doorless car, scratching his head. Thankfully, insurance companies in Vanguard City were well accustomed to the damages caused by the city's defenders.

"What the hell?" A pile of clothes lay crumpled on the sidewalk in front of Sebastian's building. I nonchalantly picked it up, scanning the streets for where he might have run off to. Somewhere in the city, there was a naked bear, waiting for his boxer-briefs to be delivered.

Unless he withheld his ability to fly, he'd have to duck somewhere and hide. The alley. I shuffled along the sidewalk, eyeing each person as I passed. It was shocking how the people of this city returned to their business, as if they hadn't almost been destroyed by a woman with evil intent.

I stepped off the sidewalk into the alley used by trash trucks to pick up the occupant's refuse. I gave a few smaller trashcans a kick, uncertain if they were big enough to hide a grown man. It wasn't until I heard a hiss that I spun about to see a dumpster.

Sebastian leaned out, showing his displeasure. Next training session, we'd look at better ways to make a grand exit and not need to hide in the alley.

I ran to him, about to thrust the pile of clothes in his hands, when I paused.

"What?"

"Nothing," I smiled, "looks like we're still going to need that shower."

13

"I'm cumming," he growled.

The warning was redundant. I could feel his girth expand as he buried his cock in my ass. Braced against the wall of his shower, there was nowhere to go, pinned between the tile and his cock. It was a marvelous place to be trapped.

Before he finished panting, while still buried inside, he pulled me away from the wall. Sliding one hand around my waist, he gripped my hard on, while the other found a home in the center of my chest. He continued a light rocking motion, reminding me he wasn't done.

I bit my lip as his hand worked up and down the length of my shaft. Circling it with his pointer and thumb, the jerking turned rapid. He shoved deeper, and as his cock signaled its last hurrah, I shot my load on the shower wall.

With a shift of his hips, he slid free, and thankfully so. Everybody thinks a big cock is better, but on the receiving end, it can be touch and go. Perhaps if I hadn't cum, I'd be able to take a second round from him, but now? He'd be playing with himself alone before I let him fuck me again tonight.

"Time for bed?" he whispered in my ear before kissing my neck.

"In just a minute. Somebody just made a mess again."

"What can I say?" he gave my ass a squeeze. "I enjoy knowing you're full of my cum."

I couldn't deny his logic. It was hot. In theory. But the last thing I needed was his cum running down my leg. We were a bit too early in whatever *this* was to stain his carpets. I had to save something for the second trip to his loft.

I finished washing up before grabbing a towel and drying off. I wandered from the bathroom into the bedroom and, other than the location in the city, the money at Sebastian's disposal wasn't noticeable at first glance. But the more I studied the items lining his dresser, the collection of watches in a display box, or the expensive cologne, it was obvious he was a minimalist *and* wealthy.

"Feeling better?" he asked.

"Yeah, I needed that." My cheeks warmed. "Shower wasn't half bad either."

Sebastian dropped his towel and fell back onto the bed, his legs hanging over the side. It was too early to call it a night, but I wasn't going to turn down an opportunity to curl up and be close. I crawled onto the bed, so I lay perpendicular to him, my head resting on his stomach.

When he reached out, using his fingers to trace circles through my chest hair, I nearly purred. I could have laid there for the rest of the night, my head rising and falling every time he took a breath. Handsome man, check. Great sex, double check. Somebody willing to let me use them as a pillow? Check. Check. Check.

"That was impressive."

"You've got a great ass. What can I say?"

I rolled over, propping myself on my elbows. "Appreciated. I meant what you did with Wraith. That was impressive. Cobalt and Zipper were knocked out of the fight by her, and you held your ground. If it wasn't for you, who knows what would have happened to Vincent."

"He deserved whatever she was going to do to him."

The words lacked emotion, a strung together sentence built with icicles. I didn't want to poke the bear and put us in jeopardy, but I needed to know the cause for the callous words.

"Vincent is a jerk, I get it. But death? That's more than a little harsh."

He rolled onto his side, so that we were looking at one another upside down. I don't know if it was the closeness, or the fact we were naked in his bed, but this felt far more intimate than getting railed in the shower.

"Men like him..." his eyes rolled back in his head. "When I lived in Southland, we'd see people like him. They were these rich guys who strolled through the poor side of town like they were impressing us."

"That seems a bit arrogant, even for the wealthy."

"They believe they're Gods. Worse than that, they want people to fall over themselves, desperate to worship at the altar of capitalism."

It was hard to sympathize with a man who wore a suit that was more than my rent. I'm also pretty sure we were lying in a king-sized bed with feather-top duvet. He might have once been a poor kid from Southland, but that identity had been buried underneath dollar signs.

"It drove me nuts. We barely had food on our table, and they were driving cars that could have paid for one of the good private schools. But what makes me angry," his lip tightened in a sneer, "it worked. People flocked to them just for a chance to bask in their opulence."

"You think Vincent is like one of those idiots?" It was hard to deny what a horrific boss he had been. I could easily see him flaunting his success, the same success he robbed from the pockets of his employees.

"I know the type. They deserve exactly what's coming to them."

"But you jumped in and saved the day? You did the right thing."

I was about to confess that I only ran into danger so

that he'd save me. Perhaps saving Vincent had been a byproduct of my recklessness, but at least Sebastian had gotten a taste of being a hero.

"If she offed him, I don't think anybody would have missed the jerk. I wanted nothing to do with that, but," he rested a hand on my cheek, "I wasn't going to let anything to happen to you."

I bit my bottom lip, chewing it as I debated confessing.

"It's brave that you tried to save him. At least one of us has the heart of a hero."

Nope, I'd take the secret to my deathbed. I grabbed the words, shoved them in a box, locked it, and buried it in a deep grave. If he knew my heroics were thinly veiled emotional manipulation, I'm not sure we'd survive the fallout.

Between Dan leaving me, ripping out my heart as he left, and the Beacon squashing my contributions, it was hard to believe I was good enough. Despite the assurances by friends, there was a black cloud wrapped around my heart that I couldn't shake. But here I was, lying in bed with the sexiest man, and despite our lifestyle differences, he chased after *me*. I couldn't put my finger on why that unnerved me.

During the trainings, our roles had been reversed. I was the veteran in the superhero world, I knew everything there was to being a superhero. Sebastian had the potential to be legendary, somebody capable of walking among the

Centurions as their equal. As a sidekick, hell, as a mentor, I wasn't just good enough. I was one of the best. But despite my guidance, Sebastian wasn't transforming into the hero I believed he could be.

Ironic that a man capable of literally vanquishing the darkness managed to add to it. Sebastian scooted across the bed, closing the gap until he planted a kiss on my lips.

There was a shimmer of light in his eyes, and, for a moment, it pierced my self-doubt, shoving them away. Whatever was developing between us, it had the ability to heal these wounds. I needed more time to reflect.

For right now, I wanted to enjoy a naked man. I returned the kiss, savoring the taste of his skin. "I could spend the night doing this, but I have a project due for Damien."

He pushed off, sitting upright. "Right, suppose I should get dressed."

"Don't go talking crazy." As he stood, he flexed his muscles, and I nearly lunged. Those broad shoulders and the grooves of his collarbone leading to his chest... "Right, get dressed or I'll never get work done."

He laughed, striking a pose before grabbing his lounge pants. "What are we going to do about food? I could cook. How do you feel about Vietnamese food?"

"Of course, you cook Vietnamese," I conceded.

He paused, thinking he was being sly as his eyes

scanned up and down my body. "Whatever makes your life easier, I need to get cracking."

As he put on a shirt, the blood moved from my groin to my brain, and I could think clearly again. It was time to earn myself a position at Revelations. This was the opportunity to prove to myself that I was good enough.

I just had to not fuck it up.

14

"Griffin." Bernard rested his elbows on the table, leaning forward. His eyes narrowed as he threatened to penetrate my skull with laser vision. No, Bernard didn't have that superpower, at least not that I knew of. His powers were more about brute strength. Oh, and he had a knack for smelling a secret.

"Griffin, did you get laid again?"

Xander and Alejandro shifted their seats, adding their eyes to the stare down. Normally, I'd have flipped them off or rolled my eyes. Crap, the moment I questioned my actions, they leaned forward until Alejandro touched my wrist.

"He got laid." Alejandro's ability to detect sex bordered on being a superpower.

"No, it's not that," Bernard's lips stretched until his

smile bordered on sinister. "It's the same guy. Griffin, are you dating?"

I prayed Dr. Quake would split the floor under the coffee shop and it'd swallow me whole. Try as I might to resist their combined efforts, my cheeks betrayed me. I hated when they turned their attention on my love life. Historically, it was to commiserate with a kind, "Maybe next time" or "You're too good for him." After a while, it got patronizing. But this time, the story didn't end with my heart broken.

"That Sebastian guy?" At least Xander wanted mundane details.

"I don't care about who, how big? Cut? Uncut? Oh, please tell he was uncut. Bottom? Juicy — "

"Whoa, down boy," Bernard patted Alejandro on the shoulder. "We don't *need* to know if he's a shooter or not."

There was no point in lying, even if it was lying by omission. The rules of brunch demanded honesty. I straightened in my chair, taking a sip of coffee while I eyed each of them. Yes, I wanted them sitting on the edge of their chairs before I dished the details. It was only fitting to make them suffer a little. For once, I held the cards, and they were some seriously handsome cards.

"It's sex, not state secrets!" Xander blurted out, smacking the table louder than necessary.

"Yes, it's Sebastian. I think it's a thing. We haven't gotten to that conversation, but I'm hopeful." I was about to reveal his secret about the Legos, but I decided that was a detail for just me. "And just so you know, Alejandro, he's a stud in the bedroom."

"That's our boy." Alejandro patted me on the cheek. "Glad to hear somebody realized you're a catch."

"Last night," I shifted uncomfortably, but I couldn't resist, "let's just say he injected some pep in my step."

"Did he just make a sex joke?" Alejandro rested the back of his hand on my forehead. "He's not sick."

Okay, now I rolled my eyes. They were never going to let me live this down. If they weren't my friends, I'm pretty sure I'd hate them. Bring on the ribbing. I'd survive their best attempts to turn my face red.

"We should probably take his temperature." Xander reached for the red duffle bag filled with his medical gear. "Oh wait, I don't think I have a meat thermometer."

"Guys," Bernard waived them off, "leave him alone. It's mean to mess with somebody who is getting fucked stupid on a regular basis."

"Bernard," my jaw dropped, "you too?"

"Yup." He straightened his back as he stroked his moustache. "Good for you, kid."

The joking didn't faze me, but a simple compliment from Bernard made my cheeks burn. It had been a while since I came to the coffee shop with a victory in my pocket. I didn't want to brag, but I was glad they understood how much this one meant to me.

"Chad," Bernard yelled, "get Griffin a coffee. We're celebrating him getting laid twice... by the same guy."

Dead. I wanted them all dead. I didn't know how, but I would get them back. If it required me to make a pact with an ancient Norse God and swearing my allegiance to the underworld, I would have my revenge.

Bernard's smile stretched until he bared his teeth. Best friend, or arch-nemesis, only time would tell.

He lifted his coffee, saluting me. "So, what's everybody up to today?"

I let out a yawn. Three coffees had done nothing to shake the need for sleep. Reaching for the door, I gave my head a light shake, loosening the relentless cobwebs. The Vietnamese food had been enjoyable, and Sebastian wasn't joking about his culinary skill, but I should have left before that. No, instead I let my affection override common sense and I spent half the night working on the design package for Damien.

With a little time to kill, I needed the opinion of the one artistic person I trusted. It just so happened that Lydia was also more jolting than any amount of caffeine. I had barely cracked the door when her screech filled the comic bookstore.

"Griffin!"

Yup, I was right. With one screeching word, my heart thumped, and my ears rang. I stepped inside the store to see that she had already changed hair color since I saw her last. Now an electric green ponytail stood nearly a foot straight off her head. The font on her black sleeveless hoodie had a matched her hair, reading a bold, "My Sword is Bigger than Your Dick."

"Did you read it? Please tell me you read it. If you didn't read it, you need to leave."

"Do you wake up like this? Or does it require drugs?"

"Jerk," she leaned over the counter with the cash register. "What did you think?"

Every time I stumbled over my design last night, I paused to read a few pages of *Die. Hero. Die.* If I had entered the store without reading it, there was no way Lydia would avoid spoilers.

"It was good, really good. I have to say, I didn't see the twist coming."

"Right? It's literally in the title. They didn't mean him dying physically, they meant the death of a hero. That's ballsy."

"You think?"

"He literally tore the heart out of his girlfriend's chest."

I shook my head. "He did it to save the people in the building from dying. There wasn't a choice, either kill her or kill them. He sacrificed her for the better—"

"Wait," she shook her head, waving at me to stop talking. "You're defending what he did? A hero doesn't kill people. That's part of the code."

"I don't think it's—"

"Are we about to have a fight? I feel like we're going to fight."

"We're going to fight if you don't let me speak." She straightened her back, tracing a line down the center of her body as she attempted to find her Zen. Lydia might look calm on the outside, but it was obvious there was a turbulent storm brewing just beneath the surface.

"Speak."

"He was put into a situation without a win. No matter what he did, it was going to damage the reader's pristine image of the hero. I think the artist was saying being a hero isn't that easy. Nothing is black and white, it's a muddy grey."

Lydia massaged the bridge of her nose. When I tried to talk, she let out a long shush while holding up a finger. Considering the tongue lashing I received during brunch, I grew suspicious that everybody in my life believed they *were* the queen of drama.

"Sorry, I needed to collect myself before I hurled Centurion action figures at your head." Had it been Xander, I'd have called his bluff. Lydia didn't play at threats. Last thing I needed was an action figure of Bernard pelting me in the forehead.

"Hero is given two options," she started. "Kill his girlfriend, or let hostages be murdered. There's no win to be had, right?"

"Agreed." I picked up a little plastic Bernard dressed as Sentinel. "So the logical—"

"No," Lydia barked. "You and I, normal people, we pick the smallest body count. You and I are *not* heroes. We're people. So, let's try this again. You have two options. What do you do?"

We often fought about comics, and once she got an idea in her head, she wouldn't relent. She struck the hero of the comic down because he didn't make the correct decision. But sometimes there simply aren't choices that result in good or bad. Life wasn't a comic book; it was infinitely more complicated. This wasn't a black or white, yes or no question.

"He did the right thing." I stood firm.

Having a tiny Bernard chucked against my forehead hurt as much as I anticipated. Before I found the dent, Lydia launched into her tirade.

"Superheroes don't get to pick the lesser of two evils. Evil is evil. He should have gone with option C."

"But you said—"

"They're superheroes, they don't care what I said. He could have gone back in time. He could have frozen the room. Heroes don't get the luxury of living in a muddy gray."

I knew we were discussing a comic book, a great one at

that, but her words stung. If I didn't know better, I'd have thought she was talking about Sebastian. Was I justifying bad behavior because I liked the man? He attempted to bypass the questions by hiding his abilities, but did that mean he was picking an evil, even if only a tiny one? The question would nag at me all day.

"Are you okay?" she asked. "You're a million miles away."

She snapped her fingers, knocking me out of my thoughts. "Sorry about that. It's a work thing eating at me. I came in here to get your opinion on a spread I'm present-ing. Hoping it's enough to land me the job."

"We'll put a pin in this conversation," her eyes narrowed, "but don't think we're done."

I reached into my messenger bag. Once I had the port-folio in hand, I hesitated, worried Lydia was about to tear apart my design. Normally I wouldn't care. I had grown used to brutal critiques, but none with stakes this high.

"Hand it over!" she yelled.

I thrust it into her waiting hands. She started flipping until she reached the last page. While she inspected my work, I wandered away from the counter, thumbing through the comics on the shelves. An entire wall of her shop held new release comics, hundreds by my estimate. Perhaps once I landed this job, I could afford to start reading them again. Loving comics generally meant being poor.

"Want my honest opinion? Or do you want me to sugar coat it, so you feel good going into your meeting?"

My heart sank.

"Griff, I'm messing with you." She spun the portfolio around, showing off my work. "You have a visual punch to make the page flippers stop. You've butchered the article in places and pushed the design elements to the forefront. There's no way somebody is going to see this and not think that a designer stood at the helm."

"But is it good?"

She closed it, sliding it across the counter. "You don't have a thing to worry about. It's good, bordering on great. You just need to be ready to stand behind your decisions and throw down with anybody who says otherwise."

Leave it to Lydia to say the exact thing I needed to hear.

15

———

"BUTTON YOUR SHIRT." DAMIEN'S WORDS HELD A TINGE OF annoyance. "This isn't a frat house."

With Lydia's words guiding me, I had stepped into the lion's den, ready to fight. But today, something had irritated the creature, and he was more than happy to direct his anger toward me.

"With a little time at the gym, you'd be a powerhouse. It might be something to consider."

Two fast jabs at my appearance and I hadn't even pulled the portfolio from my bag. I had been prepared to roll in like a storm and sell my design, to explain how it would be the perfect addition to his magazine. He quickly knocked the wind from my sail. Damien Vex had come across as sly before, but now, he had slipped into sadistic.

I needed his attention to shift from my person to my

work. There were only so many attacks I could handle in the first two minutes of our meeting before I started a gym membership and burned my entire wardrobe.

"I have the design package you wanted."

Damien held out his hand without another word. Something about his attitude rubbed me the wrong way. If he wasn't my last opportunity for a job designing for a superhero publication, I might have taken my efforts elsewhere. This domineering attitude reminded me of the man who threatened Bossman in his own office. I had to remind myself that I was playing with dynamite, and it came with a short fuse.

I pulled the portfolio from my bag, opened it to the design, and set it in his hands. He eyed the pages as he walked around his desk, sitting in his chair while I awkwardly stood in the middle of his office. Closing the top button of my shirt, I took a step forward until I was hovering over his desk.

It only required a few seconds to inspect the design, but he studied it like a work of art. Minutes passed as he scanned the pages. His hand moved to his face, pointer finger hovering just above his lip. I counted his blinks, looking for any sign of approval from his perfectly manufactured body language.

When we hit the ten-minute mark, I convinced myself that Damien dragged out the process as a form of torture. Even the most astute designer would have picked apart the work by now. My muscles twitched, forcing me to shift my weight from one leg to the other. I was only sixty seconds from grabbing the portfolio and storming out of his office.

"It has potential."

I let out a long sigh. "I appreciate—"

"I didn't say it was good."

I had professors like him. They lured you in with a compliment to drop the hammer. Damien thought he was playing a skillful game, but he hadn't gone to design school. This was par for the course, and now that we were focused on my work and not on me, I was in my element. When it came to our work, designers have skin far thicker than the average person.

"Your concept is complete garbage. I'm not entirely sure you understand what we do here." He closed the book, taking his time as he leaned back in his chair. "Your puff piece about a hero discovering their abilities is tired and, frankly, a laughable cliché. But I understand, you're not a journalist."

He understood, but he didn't miss the opportunity to sink the blade into my chest.

"I understand the Beacon publishes articles like this. Their determination to make heroes into idols for mankind to worship is cute, but it's dangerous. Our readers want to see the secrets behind these supposed Gods."

"I understand."

"I'm not sure you do. I can guess that you're a guy who

grew up reading about these people in comics. They were a bit of escapism from a rough childhood. It lets you turn a blind eye to the reality, but Revelations is about discovering the truth. Just because they have powers, it doesn't make them heroes."

I stared at my shoes, digesting his words. The tips of my toes were resting on a black line in his carpet, a giant geometric print that maintained the dark modern theme of his office. My left shoelace had come undone, and I was surprised Damien hadn't managed to spot the imperfection. I debated dropping to a knee to tie it, just to break the tension.

He might have been speaking about the magazine and their mission statement, but his words poked at a growing concern. Had I been wrong about Sebastian? When I discovered he had powers, I rushed to the image of him being a hero protecting the city from villains. I thought I could help mold him into this pinnacle of righteousness, but since we started training, my faith had wavered. Now, Damien preached as if he read my mind and if he were right, Sebastian's powers meant nothing. He had been willing to save me... that should count for something, right? I tried to ignore Damien's cryptic monologue.

"The design is adequate. I think it gets a bit sloppy at times. Just because you know a particular technique, it doesn't mean you have to use it. There is power in minimalism."

Damien gestured to his office, a reminder that with the correct lighting, appropriate colors, and carefully placed items, you could set a stage. I was used to Bossman's inability to understand how visuals improved the magazine, a completely right-brained individual. I had assumed Damien was the same, but if he was the one who designed his office, perhaps he was more skilled than I gave him credit.

"The question is," he laced his fingers together, pointers pushed against the bottom of his chin, "does it warrant a second chance?"

His eyes turned from the portfolio to me. There were no beams of red light shooting from them, but it still felt as if he were burrowing through my chest. Damien held all the cards. I couldn't go crawling back to the Beacon and expect Vincent to show me mercy, even if I had saved his life. Right now, a second chance to impress this overly critical tyrant was all I had.

"Do you understand what I'm looking for?" he asked.

The reality of superpowers, and how having them didn't mean they were the heroes we painted them. Part of my childhood shattered as I nodded my head.

"I do."

Damien pushed my portfolio across his desk. "One more chance. Put aside these childish expectations. Comic books are for kids and men unable to get laid."

I wanted to growl that I had gotten laid and read comics

yesterday. I wanted to ensure that he understood being a geek was providing me with plenty of sex. But I bit my tongue, and I felt myself sink into a hole, burying pieces of my identity.

"Next time we meet, I want you looking the role of a Revelations employee. We have standards and taking riffraff off the street isn't in our nature. Consider a suit, maybe a shave, and then I won't be distracted looking at your work."

I snatched my portfolio from his desk. I had seen a dozen employees walking toward his office, and I kicked myself for not noticing the dress code. If that wasn't enough, I felt as if I had squandered my first impression and now, I worked at a deficit. It would take something seriously impressive to pull myself out of this hole.

A part of me died as I nodded my head.

"Thank you."

"I see something special in you, Mr. Smith," he said. "Perhaps rough around the edges, but we can remake you into the best version of yourself."

With a wave, he signaled the meeting had come to an end. I didn't even warrant a farewell. He simply turned to a stack of papers while I saw myself out. The feelings of insecurity crept in, and I could see my chance to prove myself slipping. Every time I thought I'd freed myself of the self-doubt, made a step forward in cementing my success, I tumbled from the ladder to start over again.

I'd joke about it, but it hurt.

I scoured the offices and cubicles on the walk to the elevator to see if I could spot Sebastian. After the tongue-lashing from Damien, I could use a friendly face. With the uneasy feeling brewing in my chest, a hug would do wonders.

Everybody dressed as snappy as Damien. From the designers in their concept meeting to the sales staff on the phones, they looked as if they shopped at the same store. I don't think I owned anything half as nice. While it might seem overkill to have a strict dress code, I had to complement their attention to the branding of Revelations. I'd never be able to see somebody in a black dress shirt and dark red tie and not think they worked here.

I reached the elevator without spotting Sebastian. I checked my phone to see if he might have texted me a "good luck" or "you've got this." My confidence had imploded, whittled away with one dig after another. The lack of communication piled on top of the sense of inadequacy. It was illogical, but the heart didn't tend to think of the world in terms of logic.

Pushing the button, I watched as the digital readout signaled the elevator speeding upward. To my right, hidden just outside my peripheral vision, a woman waited patiently for the doors to open.

I turned and gave her a slight smile. Her jet-black hair had been pulled back into a carefully crafted bun. She returned a smile, the one where a woman is being polite but secretly deciding if I was going to be one of *those* men.

The elevator opened, and I stepped to the side.

"After you."

"Thank you." She stepped on the elevator and gave me the once over. "You're not one of ours?"

"Interviewing with Mr. Vex. I'm after one of the design positions for the magazine."

"A word of advice. Mr. Vex is particular about his employees. You're going to need to fix this," she motioned to all of me, "if you hope to impress him." She didn't have to elaborate. Damien had been abundantly clear.

"Thanks." It's the polite thing to say, but the last thing I needed was another person drilling into my appearance. If I could have any superpower right now, it'd be to turn myself invisible and dart away unseen.

"How did you hear about the position?" The doors hung open for a second longer before shutting.

"Sebastian Taylor."

"Oh," she gave me the up and down before adding, "Ohhh."

I hadn't talked to Sebastian about workplace etiquette. For all I knew, he wasn't out at work, and I didn't want to place him in an awkward position with his co-workers. But obviously, she knew him well enough to know that he had a type and I fit.

"Yeah, I met him while working at the Beacon."

"I see." She rested her hands in front of her, one over the other. The position made her chest even more pronounced. I couldn't imagine being a woman in a ruthless industry, but if she chose to weaponize her sex, then more power to her.

"I've known Sebastian for years." Her tone had shifted. The statement had an edge of condescension to it. If this conversation was about to be like all the others today, I braced myself for daggers.

"He's a good guy. He clawed his way out of Southlands and made something of himself."

A compliment? I hadn't been prepared for—

"He's a valuable asset to Revelations. His creativity is part of what keeps this magazine afloat and he's proven his worth. I don't mean to judge..." Of course, she did. Nobody ever prefaces a flattering statement. It only happens when they're about to tear through you. "But you're playing out of your league. Sebastian, Revelations, this is for the best."

I did the only logical thing.

"Thanks." Yup, even as the woman was raking me over the coals, reminding me that I wasn't good enough at my job or at my relationship, I thanked her.

"I'm sure you're good at whatever it is you do. But

Sebastian has a higher calling, and any distractions are..." she paused, trying to bait me as she pretended to search for a harsh word, "fleeting."

"I appreciate the advice..." I hadn't even caught the woman's name. "Your name?" If I needed to discuss it with Sebastian, I didn't want him mistaking her for one of the other dozen women in near identical clothes.

"Rebecca, head of Marketing for Revelations" she turned, holding out her hand as the elevator slowed.

My mother would be proud of me minding my manners, but right now I couldn't decide if I wanted to cry or smack her. After a day of being told I wasn't good enough, that I wasn't capable of playing with the "big boys," I put away my civility and did the nastiest thing I could think of. I ignored her hand.

The ding sounded like a victory chime. I'd deal with these feelings later, but for now, I reveled, beating her at the dismissive game. As the doors opened, I stepped from the elevator, not caring if a gentleman should wait. When she didn't follow, I realized I had been played. Rebecca never needed to leave the building. She merely wanted to share her version of advice and leave me to pick up the pieces.

I turned, ready to curse at the woman. The grin said everything. She had emerged victorious in this game of chess. Her hand spun about a metal necklace, the end of it vanishing into her cleavage. My lip raised in a snarl as I sorted through a list of vulgar insults.

As the doors shut, she tugged on the necklace. At the end, nestled against her flawless skin, I caught a glimpse of a jewel mostly hidden from sight, a green pendant.

Rebecca vanished as doors closed and the elevator raced upward. She might as well have been standing in front of me. The image of her burned into my retina. This woman, a vile one at that, had just shared a dirty little secret.

Rebecca was a supervillain.

16

I checked my phone for the millionth time in the last hour. No new messages, no texts. I clicked the corner, double checking that I was able to get a signal despite being in the back of the restaurant. I flipped back to my text messages. Nothing.

"I get fashionably late, but..."

I turned on my camera and gave myself the once over. Neatly trimmed hair, manicured goatee, even a bit of moisturizer to make sure I looked my best. The facial regimen might have gone overboard, but I wanted to make a statement tonight. I snapped a photo so I could prove to the guys that I cleaned up pretty well when motivated.

I inspected the knot of my tie. It wasn't perfect, a little larger than it should have been, but I didn't dare fuss it with anymore. I gave it a slight tug, loosening it enough that it didn't catch on the stubble under my chin.

"Not too shabby Griffin."

I put my phone down. I had never been to the restaurant before, but it was considered one of the nicest in the area, and only a few blocks from Sebastian's loft. I figured after a long day at work, he wouldn't want to traipse across town. If dinner went well, I hoped my tie would be hanging on his doorknob by the end of the night.

The candle on the table flickered. At first, I thought it was fancy because each table held a vase filled with flowers arranged that morning. But the more I examined the decor, the more I realized how upscale it was. The dark wood along the walls softened the industrial feel of the metal along the bar. It was swankier than any joint in the Ward. I had grown accustomed to plastic counter tops made for easy cleaning.

It was a narrow space, with a group of tables in the front, near the window overlooking the street. The bar occupied the middle, running the length of the space with metal barstools with wide, dark wood seats. The liquor on display behind the bartender was perfectly spaced out, light from beneath, making the bottles glow and providing most of the light in this area. I had been given a seat in the back, near a custom wooden divider that hid the entrance into the kitchen.

From here, I had the opportunity to watch all the

patrons as they went about their meals. An older couple ate in silence, consumed by their food. I imagined she was his second wife, somebody he met at the club. Their courtship had been rushed as she attempted to climb the social ladder and he wanted the prestige of landing a bride twenty-years his junior.

Not far from them, a trio swished wine around in their glasses, drinking the amber liquid deeply. All three wore suits, and I couldn't quite decide if their evening out was for leisure or business. When the waiter returned, he had brought another bottle of wine, and without asking, exchanged it for the empty one.

One of the men said something, holding out his glass. The waiter looked petrified as he apologized for whatever faux pas he had committed. Though he had brought them another bottle, apparently, he had forgotten to pour them their next glass. I couldn't help but roll my eyes, astonished at the entitled behavior of the patron.

"I'd pop him one in the jaw," I muttered.

Now that I had seen a single transgression, I searched for more. The bartender brought a drink to a woman wearing more diamonds than I'd ever afford in my lifetime. As he placed the martini glass on the bar, she reached out, her hands grazing up the length of his forearm. She held him in place, lingering far longer than should be appropriate. The forced smile had been well-rehearsed, but he couldn't fake it in the eyes. To maintain his employment, he embodied the flirt, whether he liked it or not.

"This is so not me." I loosened my tie, convinced I had made a fool of myself. I silently cursed Damien's name while unfastening my top button. I was far more content grabbing a milk shake and burger than whatever was on this menu. Who in their right mind ate pigeon? Perhaps I was always going to be a guy from the Ward, low brow and unsophisticated.

I froze as my phone rattled along the table. After an hour of waiting for him to open the door, I assumed it couldn't be good news. It vibrated again, short with an abrupt second shake. A text message, two of them to be precise. If I didn't flip it over and read his message, there was still hope that I'd catch him speaking to the hostess.

Cautiously, I reached for the phone, glancing to the front of the restaurant, hoping that he might ask where I was seated. A shallow inhale and I flipped it over, but at this angle, I couldn't make out the message. One step closer to confirming my fears.

Purgatory wasn't the middle ground between Heaven and Hell. It was a hell that prayed on hope. I picked up the phone and flipped it open to read my messages.

Two texts from Sebastian.

I sank into my chair, pulling at my tie until it slid from around my neck. I shoved it in my pocket as I reread the message, worried I might have misread his text. Even after the third time, there was nothing salvageable. I hovered over the last line of the first text.

"Head of marketing pulled me into a meeting."

Sebastian had bailed on plans with me because of Rebecca. At least as Wraith, I could understand her motivation. According to Lydia, if you weren't good, then you were bad. It made sense. But her twisted game with Sebastian? That would drive a wedge between us. What did she have to gain? Worse than that, he waited an hour, letting me sit here in this posh restaurant looking like a fool.

"Sir," I jumped at the sudden appearance of the waiter. He bent at the waist, whispering as he spoke. "I hate to do this, but if you're not going to order—"

"No, no, that's fine. I understand."

"I apologize for the inconvenience." I pulled the napkin from my lap, dropping it on the table. I reached into my back pocket, pulling out my wallet, opening it and handing the man a twenty. He quietly accepted, trying to keep the situation from becoming more awkward.

I grabbed my phone off the table and moved through the restaurant. The bartender looked up from polishing a glass and I could swear even the older couple's eyes followed me. The hostess opened the door, giving me a slight bow as I left.

Turning right, I walked to the end of the building, where it split into an alley. Stepping off the sidewalk, I pressed my back to the wall. I banged the back of my skull against the concrete, fighting to keep myself afloat.

I lost the battle and started to spiral.

The tears gathered in the corner of my eyes, and I stopped resisting. A tightness formed in my chest, and I struggled to pull at the buttons, feeling it constrict. Even once I managed to unbutton half the shirt, I struggled to draw breath, and each time I managed, it came in a ragged sob.

This had been the breaking point. I had defended Sebastian to Lydia, and then I endured Damien's volley of demeaning remarks. Each jagged remark drew blood, only a few drops, but they left stains. As Rebecca attacked, she had gone for the jugular, and I thought her a vile bitch. But she had been right.

I lifted my phone. There should have been another text, one apologizing. It should have complimented me for stepping outside my comfort zone and making reservations at a restaurant that I'd have never gone to if it weren't for Sebastian. There should have been a cute remark about making it up to me. Instead, I reread the second message.

"Maybe another time?"

I slowed as I walked along the pavement in front of the Hideout. After nearly three miles of collecting my thoughts, I hadn't gotten any closer to shaking the wretched feeling making itself at home in my chest.

I had considered calling Xander, but I couldn't handle the waves of anger once he found out what happened. Alejandro would be off to work, and somehow, I feel like I would have let Bernard down. While they were a great group of friends, the sense of loneliness was palpable.

I stopped walking for a moment, trying to gather my thoughts. If they strayed too far, bending and warping at the request of self-doubt, I'd start crying again. At this point, I'm not sure it mattered. There was a good chance there were no tears left for tonight's ordeal.

"Griffin?"

There was no way to speak without sounding pathetic. I must look a mess, because the moment the light caught my face, Chad was already out the door, arm around my back, guiding me into the coffee shop. There was no fight left in me, and I moved forward as if being guided through a dream.

The only lights that remained on were over the coffee bar. I had never been in the shop without dozens of patrons sipping their hot beverages. He steered me toward one of the bar stools while he assumed his role behind the counter.

He flipped over a mug without flourish and set it in front of me. I held up my hand to protest. The last thing my anxiety needed was enough energy to rally and begin its second assault of the evening. However, as Chad ducked low behind the counter, he held up a bottle of bourbon, pouring me a healthy amount.

"I can't tell if you look good, or you look like a wreck. Where are you coming from?"

"The city." I tipped the mug so I can see the contents. There must have been five or six shots, more alcohol than I had consumed in the last six months. I had never been one for booze, but after three miles of my brain wrestling with itself and losing every match, it couldn't hurt.

I gulped the liquid, and even as it burned my throat, I swallowed another mouthful. Once the cup emptied, the taste of moss filled my mouth and my eyes widened. My sinuses had cleared, and I could breathe easy, even if the only thing I could smell was rubbing alcohol.

"You're going to feel that in an hour."

"Couldn't feel any worse." Everybody knew Chad. He always had a kind word to say, and like a psychic, he could read a room with the best of them. If a situation called for humor, there were jokes to be told, and if a patron had a bad day, he had a knack of knowing how to lift their spirits. We weren't close, but he'd assume the role if I needed.

"Do you want to talk about it?"

"Not really." Yes, I wanted to talk about it. I wanted his opinion on relationships, one of his favorite subjects. What I didn't want was another deluge of tears and snot running down my face as I lost my cool.

"When I saw you this morning, you were excited about a new—oh."

He reached across the counter, squeezing my hands. "Is it about Mr. Perfect?"

I nodded. "He stood me up."

This is where Xander would have threatened to kill him. He'd have meant it and had Sebastian not had superpowers, I might be worried. Chad didn't offer any promises of bodily harm, instead he held onto my hands. Every few seconds as space between us remained quiet, he tightened his grip, reminding me he was there.

"He's out of my league." I thought Chad might chime in to argue my point of view, but instead, he leaned against the counter, letting me speak. "He's rich, or at least my definition of rich, and he has my dream job. The loft is amazing, and he's just," I couldn't reveal his secret, no matter how hurt. "He's amazing."

"You're talking a lot about him. What about yourself?"

"Me?" I laughed, but stopped as the taste of alcohol resurfaced. "I don't have a job. I'll have to get some shit job soon to pay the rent. I have a useless college degree. How can I live up to that? I feel like I was on the receiving end of a pity date."

"Do you want to hear my opinion?"

"No," I returned a squeeze, "But you're going to tell me, anyway." I forced a smile that lasted just shy of a split second.

"Rude," he started. "You don't have a job because you're talented and those assholes at the Beacon didn't respect that. You got fired because you decided to value yourself."

"Look where self-esteem got me!" How fast did it take for alcohol to kick in? The warmth in my stomach had spread to the rest of my torso.

"It got you out of an abusive relationship. As for this man—"

"Sebastian."

Chad made a sour face. "The same goes for Sebastian. If he's not going to value you, then you have to do it."

I'm sure with a good night's sleep, I might not be teetering on the edge of emotional oblivion. If it had been an isolated incident, I might have shaken it from my shoulders. But Dan had been the first to point out my inability to succeed. Now it looked like that lack of success with work had infected my relationship as well.

"How do you know if somebody is good?"

Chad pulled his hands free. Scrunching up his face, he searched for the appropriate answer. I had seen him every day for the last few years, but I had never noticed his beard and how he squared the hair along the jawline. A literal light hung above his head, making him appear almost comical.

"I guess once you meet the right person—"

"Not good for you. Just, good."

"You're asking the hard questions tonight." He raised

the bottle of bourbon to his lips, taking a swig. "I guess that's unique to each person. But since actions speak louder than words, I think a good person is somebody who does good things."

"If they don't do good things, are they bad?"

"Griffin, did he do something to you?"

I quickly shook my head, and even after I stopped, it seemed the room didn't get the memo. "Like a superhero," I said, "if he doesn't help people, is he a bad guy?"

"Maybe? I guess that's in the eye of the beholder. Let's say, Cobalt, for instance, does something I deem good, and you say is bad. What does that make him?"

The liquor was having the desired effect. The words were bouncing about my head, but I struggled to get them out of my mouth. "But there's right and wrong, right?"

Chad shrugged. "Cobalt does plenty of things I don't agree with. The property damage? Sometimes he stops the villain but doesn't prevent a civilian from getting hurt. But I must assume he's doing what he can. He's not good, nor evil, he's Cobalt."

I could barely follow the logic. But Chad's tone was soothing, kind, and free of the judgement I received all day.

"You have a crush on him?" I couldn't help but smile. I tried poking him in the chest, but my depth perception had fallen victim to bourbon, and I jabbed at empty air.

"Have you seen him in that suit? Rawr. He's a sexy man."

I couldn't argue with the logic. No, really, I was too drunk to put up a fight. At this point, anything Chad said would need to be treated as gospel.

"I'm drunk."

"Yes—yes you are. Let me flip off the lights and I'll walk you home."

"You're good people, Chad. I want you to know that. Good people. You're like the best people."

He vanished toward the back of the coffee shop. The lights blinked off, and I was left sitting in the dark. Did his stools wobble on their own? He might need to fix that before a patron fell off.

"Let's get you home."

He took me by the arm, guiding me toward the door. I leaned on him, struggling to keep myself upright. "You're good people." It was the closest thing to a compliment my brain could muster.

"You too, Griffin. You're the best people."

Thanks.

17

———

Wraith's hiss filled my ear. "You'll never be good enough for Sebastian."

I couldn't recall how I got to the bridge separating the Ward from the business district of Vanguard City. It maintained some of the older charm with black streetlamps lining the sidewalk. I couldn't remember leaving my apartment, nor walking this far.

There were no shadows. Where the light touched, I could see the bridge, but when the light ended, so did the sidewalk, as if it couldn't exist in the shadows. The darkness at her control had spread far enough that I couldn't tell which direction would lead me home.

I hugged tightly to one of the lampposts, making sure I remained within its protective borders. The tendrils of black attempted to penetrate the light, smoldering each time they broke the barrier. I searched my pockets, looking for my phone. When I couldn't find the familiar square in my pants, I went into survival mode. I just had to wait for a hero to save the day.

"You can't make him a hero."

The voice didn't have an origin. The night itself spoke, stabbing at my insecurities.

"Bitch, you're going to jail."

"Tough words, human."

The whites of her eyes were visible, hovering just outside the radius of light. My back pressed tightly against the lamppost. I couldn't do anything to escape, not unless I wanted to dash into the darkness and hope I made it to the next light before she caught me.

"You can't make him a hero," she hissed. "He wanted Vincent to die. For you, human. He wanted him to die for you."

"No!" I shouted.

"You can rally against the darkness." Her face moved as close as possible before the light threatened to sear her shadowy skin. "But not when it lives in his heart."

As she stepped forward, the skin of darkness evaporated, leaving her naked except for the pendant hanging about her neck. Even without her supernatural powers, she maintained a sinister quality, an evil that came from inside.

"He's not evil." The panic made my words quiver, and even I found it hard to believe.

"You can't save the damned." Her fingers ran along the corner of my jaw, frigid to the touch. I tried to pull away, but the lamppost refused to budge. Rebecca's fingers traced down my chest and I watched as her nail left a trail of black.

"I can save him," I whimpered.

She leaned forward. The black of her lipstick shimmered in the light as she placed her lips against mine. My body froze until she threw her head back, cackling at my discomfort. The same frigid sensation on my chest spread from lips, and I had no doubt she used it to infect me.

"Pathetic!" she yelled into the night. She stepped back, letting the shadows wrapped around the soft white of her skin. "He's not coming to save you."

I rubbed my face, trying to scrape away at whatever she did. My hands were covered in a liquid black. It spread, running along my skin as if it were alive, swallowing me one inch at a time.

My limbs surrendered, and I collapsed on the sidewalk. I couldn't stop Wraith. I would settle for any hero to come to my rescue, but deep inside, I knew there was only one I wanted. But Wraith spread doubt even more infectious than the darkness. As she pushed back the light, the tendrils latched onto my legs. I had my confirmation.

The white eyes vanished, her voice coming from the night itself. "You're not worth saving."

I kicked, flailing my arms to keep the succubus at bay. In the darkness, she tightened about my legs, refusing to let go. My hand smashed something nearby, and I froze at the sound of glass breaking.

"Hello?" I wasn't on the bridge. The fan overhead whirred, blowing cool air from the air conditioning. I reached down to my legs and found myself trapped in the twists of my sheet. I continued kicking with my legs, growing aggravated at its refusal to let go.

"Get the fuck off," I yelled.

I scooted up the bed, resting a hand on my chest. My heart continued thumping, speeding along as if it were making a last ditched effort to finish a marathon. The room spun, the effects of the booze determined to stick with me until the end. Every time I blinked, the light coming in the window vanished and my pulse quickened. I panicked, searching my nightstand until I found my phone. Pressing the screen, the flashlight filled the room.

"It's just a nightmare."

Rebecca attempting to kill me might have been a bad dream, but every word she hissed in my direction, those had been real. It would have been better had she crept in my window and finished the job she started. Instead of a supervillain attempting to kill me, my own brain thrusted my worst fears forward.

From the moment I met Sebastian, I had stumbled over my words, making a fool of myself. He was a fantasy, somebody I could eye from across the room and wonder, "What if?" I hadn't expected to get a second chance to talk to him. But more than that, I hadn't expected him to be interested.

He had made it clear where I fell. He had bailed on dinner, leaving me to make a fool of myself. Worse than that, he didn't even think it deserved an apology. Once again, I had tried to rise above my station, only to be knocked down.

Sebastian didn't come without baggage, but part of me hoped between the two of us, we'd have a matching set. I had been avoiding the conversation with myself, trying to ignore the cold look in his eyes when Wraith threatened Vincent. The hero who rescued me wouldn't let even the biggest jerk be slaughtered by the witch of darkness. If I hadn't put myself in danger, I don't know if Sebastian would have saved the day. For me, he'd challenge her, but it wasn't enough to save *just* me.

I pulled the sheet free, hurling it across the room. There was no point in going back to sleep, not when my brain fixated on Rebecca's condescending smirk. The next time I came across the woman, I'd give her a piece of my mind. She had struck a nerve, and I wanted to strike her back just the same.

I might be able to live with Sebastian not being the perfect hero. There were plenty of anti-heroes in comic books who came around to do the right thing when it mattered. But him being close to a villain? Not just co-workers, but friends? I couldn't excuse that. This battle couldn't be won.

It was time to face the truth, to stop pretending. If I laid it on the table and forced him to choose, I wouldn't win. It wasn't the first ultimatum I'd have lost in recent memory. Every time I gathered the courage to speak up, to defend myself, the world reminded me I wasn't enough. I wasn't good enough to keep my job, and I certainly wasn't good enough to keep Sebastian.

I let out a sob, burying my face in my hands. The water-works had started again. Confessing that I was a failure stung. It wasn't fair. I tried to do my best, but it never seemed to make a difference. Once again, I was falling short. I let the crying continue for the next few minutes, purging the self-pity from my system.

I leaned my head back, banging it against the head-board, hoping the quick bursts of pain could pull my mind from the dark place. When that didn't work, I grabbed a pillow, sinking my face into the soft material. It might have worked, soaking up the mess that was my face, but some-where between the threads, Sebastian's cologne spurred on the crying fit.

Minutes passed before the tears dried. I hadn't even started my day and already I had reached the end of my emotional rope. "Get it together."

I scoured the floor of my bedroom until I found a pair of shorts, careful to avoid the shattered glass. Wiping my running nose, I decided it was time to get away from the bed, away from the memory of him wrapped around my body and the nightmares delivered by the vile woman.

There were no more tears to shed. I did the only logical thing, shift my sorrow to anger. This wasn't my fault. I had done nothing wrong. Sebastian had allied himself with Wraith. It was *his* fault for giving me hope. If it wasn't for him showing up at my door and stepping inside my apartment, I wouldn't be swimming through an emotional wasteland.

"Asshole." I wasn't proud of the mental gymnastics needed to arrive at this conclusion, but it beat drowning. I could manage my anger; I could let it burn through my fingertips and be fine on the other side. Anything was better than feeling sad for myself.

Flipping on the light in the living room, I inspected the bathroom, cautious of any place the light overhead left a shadow. Once I had finished my rounds, I found myself staring at the painting, a dreadful reminder of my infatuation with Sebastian and a potential he'd never realize.

I had wasted hours indulging in my love of superheroes and a fantasy that would never happen. I scooped a bottle of white paint off the floor. The cap made a popping sound as I flipped it open. I hesitated, admiring my handiwork.

"You don't deserve me."

I splattered paint across the canvas. Ropes of white covered the painting, obscuring the superhero I had conjured. When the tube ran on empty, I dragged my hand across the surface, spreading until I buried the man beneath. With a second swipe, it was impossible to tell what the painting had been.

The sun broke over the horizon, casting an eerie light through the window and across the painting. As the anger pooled in my stomach, I contemplated throwing the canvas from the balcony. Sebastian didn't deserve to have his likeness preserved in acrylic. The reality of superheroes set in. They weren't these noble beings, defenders of good. Could Damien have been right?

The moment the publisher's name crossed my mind, I thought about the future, *my* future, with the company. If I didn't produce an article for the man, I'd have to fall back on some menial job and my degree would be for nothing. I needed it for myself, but having Sebastian see my success at Revelations, that didn't hurt my motivation.

The idea struck like lightning.

I traced my finger through the paint until I had drawn the outline of a man. As I stared at the man buried beneath the white, the article started to surface. I'd land the job. I'd prove I was a great designer and if I needed to reveal the truth behind a hero, I knew who to choose.

The phone vibrated.

The HeroApp™ alerted the neighborhood to another

villain's appearance. It just so happened it was the one villain I wanted to speak with. Wraith had taken to terrorizing a subway station only two stops away. I couldn't figure out her game and why she picked these targets. But lucky for me, I needed a story, and she was going to be at the heart of it.

It was time to confront a supervillain.

18

———————

Only the earliest commuters were out at this hour. The go-getters were on their way to work while the late-night employees sped toward their homes. If there had been any people in the subway station, Wraith managed to keep them silent.

I stood at the steps leading under the street, debating on if this was the smartest decision. Living in Vanguard City meant living with the reality of beings with unimaginable power, upsetting the natural order of things. Xander had shared a thousand stories about being the first medic on the scene of a superhero battle and the destruction they left in their wake.

"You can do it." Despite the positive affirmation, my feet didn't move. "You're going to prove you deserve that position." I only hoped once I got it, going out into the field would be a rarity. I was willing to get my hands dirty to land the position, but I'd be perfectly content staying in a cubicle with my computer for the duration of my tenure at Revelations.

"Prove yourself to them." But it wasn't them that I needed to impress. "You're good enough. You'll earn this job."

The first step had been the hardest. As my feet shuffled down the stairs, the musty smell of wet Earth filled my nostrils. The oppressive heat of the city transformed into a cool, moist sensation, equally gross.

Another staircase and I reached the turnstiles leading to the subway platform. The attendant had left their booth, probably running, terrified by the supervillain. There were no traces of her, none of the darkness she wielded, but the silence signaled something was wrong.

Opening the handicap gate, I snuck through, ducking behind a wide column. I hugged it closely, my face pressed against the beige tiles that lined nearly every surface of the station. The color might have been popular when it had been built, but now it made the entire space feel neglected.

"Where are you?" I whispered.

The platform covered several hundred feet, lined with benches and posters promoting a new television show. It widened near the end, where another exit led to the other side of the street above. I couldn't be sure with the dim fluorescent lighting, but I swore Wraith's signature darkness clouded the end of the platform.

I checked my phone, scrolling through the HeroApp™ to see if anybody had responded to the distress signal. Were Zipper and Cobalt back in the field after she bested them? If they were gone, it would be up to a hero outside the Ward to save the day. At this hour, I imagined most were safely tucked away in their beds.

"No, please don't hurt me."

There should be dozens of people in the station, but so far, I only heard a single voice. Wraith's victim sounded familiar, but in the cramped space, it was difficult to identify. I held my breath, as I shimmed over to the wall, trying to stay out of sight. From this angle I couldn't see them, but it meant Wraith couldn't spot me either. I needed to chance it if I was going to identify the voice.

I pushed off the wall, stepping behind another column. From here, I could see further into the alcove where Wraith held her hostage. I could only see the feet of a woman who must be kneeling on the tile.

"Shit," I mumbled. I had come here searching for the truth about Wraith. I wanted answers, but I had hoped it wouldn't put me face-to-face with a woman who had threatened me twice in the last two days. If I ignored the fact she had abilities, all that remained was a vindictive woman attempting to sabotage my life. I could handle confronting Rebecca.

I repeated the earlier maneuver, getting me one column closer to the Wraith and her victim. As I peeked around the side, I let out a gasp. I recognized the stylish hair immediately.

Sofia, Mr. Bossman's assistant.

I didn't know her well, but I couldn't let Wraith get away with this. If I had Sebastian's abilities, I would have charged in beams of light pelting her skin until she ran away or I managed to capture her. He wasted his gifts, hiding away from the world. Meanwhile, here I was putting my life on the line and the only gift I had was a sarcastic wit.

"What do you want? You can have my money, my jewelry."

Sofia pulled off her watch, tossing it at Wraith. A black tendril caught the time piece, absorbing it into the nothing. The villainess could have extorted money from Vincent or anybody who lived in his haughty high-rise. She didn't want money. Her brand of evil relied on instilling fear in her victims.

I slid my phone into my pocket, leaving the HeroApp™ open so I could feel it shake when somebody responded to the crisis. Wraith relied on the same trick as the day before, a blade forming from her arm. And stupidly, like before, I got involved.

"We meet again," I announced in my best blockbuster movie voice.

"G-G-Griffin?" Like all citizens of Vanguard, Sofia

expected a hero to swoop in and save the day. Unfortunately, she got me. Sorry, Sofia.

Wraith held her arm still as I approached. I didn't have super speed, and I could barely bench my own bodyweight, but I had something most heroes lacked. For years, I buried my nose in comic books. Now that the heroes were flesh and blood, these rags served like a college text book. I had an advanced degree in supers.

"You really should leave her alone."

Wraith laughed. "Did you develop powers? A chemical accident? Another wizard bestowing his abilities to a dim-witted human?"

Supervillains were notorious for their egos. It served as the most common motivator for why they got into the trade. I reached into my pocket, tapping the screen five times. Tap. Tap. Tap. Tap. Tap. On the fifth, it shook, and I tapped twice more. Tap. Tap. The HeroApp™ was now broadcasting a distress call, elevating the villain's appearance to a situation needing immediate superhero intervention.

"What's your game, Wraith?" I just needed her to talk, she'd buy us all the time in the world. "What made you like this?"

"Perfect, you mean? What made me powerful? Are you jealous, Griffin?"

Sofia gasped. "You know him?"

"Yeah, Rebecca and I go way back."

Wraith laughed, amused by my attempts to deter her efforts by using her mundane name. "Rebecca is a disguise, a mask I wear. I've been given unbelievable power. You wouldn't understand what it's like to be a god."

I definitely didn't, but she was about to tell me anyway. Rebecca's superiority complex required a speech that put herself on a pedestal, looking down at the insects. If Zipper had been released from the hospital, he'd be on his way. If one of the Centurions arrived, they'd make short work of this B-List villain.

"Power. Somebody this pathetic, you'd never understand. I'll dismantle this abysmal magazine one employee at a time. When it folds, I'll be there waiting. Then I'll show Damien. He'll finally see what I'm capable of."

Lady Trollsalot. Vincent. Sofia. Wraith's attacks weren't random. She had been unsuccessfully targeting employees from the Beacon. It wasn't a case of being in the wrong place at the wrong time when she attacked me that night. She was attempting to strip the Beacon of its employees. Why? Kill them so she could take it over? For the head of marketing, she certainly didn't understand how publications worked. Even with the four of us dead, Bossman would continue onward without a second thought.

"You're doing this to prove a point to Damien? Really? You want daddy's approval? This is just sad."

Okay, making her talk had worked. Perhaps insulting

her was a bad idea. But after the conversation in the elevator, I finally had leverage, and I wasn't going to let it go.

"You'd be dead if not for... Sebastian."

My jaw dropped.

I had been so consumed with myself, I hadn't thought about the night in the alley. When Sebastian had saved me, he had been all flashy and blinding. I had thought him safe, that he had blinded her, as well. If she knew who he was this entire time, then during the second fight, she knew it was him. At work, she dragged him into a meeting, and I thought it might be all about me. What if he had been added to her list of targets?

"Leave him alone," I warned.

"Or what? You'll infect me with your mediocrity?"

A puff of red smoke appeared between us, and a woman emerged. The black and white leather had seen better days, an unfortunate side effect of being an active super. Whoever tailored these suits couldn't keep up with the wear and tear.

Slipstream, a teleporter from the city with the ability to travel between dimensions. My distress beacon had been answered.

"Somebody need an exit?"

Rhetorical hero dialogue. It wasn't the best tagline, but at least she didn't strike a pose as she said it. She put a hand on Sofia's shoulder and a cloud of red smoke swallowed them both. Poof, gone, hopefully somewhere safe.

"It's just you and—"

The cloud appeared next to Wraith, and I silently cheered as Slipstream's fist connected with the villain's jaw. The tendrils of black shot forward, ready to pierce the hero's body armor. Before they got close, she vanished again.

"Fight me!" Wraith let the anger fuel her screams.

Slipstream emerged from another puff directly in front of me. With a wink, she wrapped her arms around my torso, shoving me back. We fell, but instead of hitting the ground, the smoke cleared, and we were on a street two blocks away from the subway.

"Stay safe. Have to go beat the snot out of that woman."

Like magic, she vanished in a puff of red smoke. I savored the image of Slipstream landing a punch. If she didn't get in a few more licks, I'd be upset. With my luck, Wraith had already vanished, like she had done previously. It seemed unless she had the upper hand, she was quick to retreat.

No matter the outcome, the risk had paid off. I had everything I needed for Damien's article. He wanted the story behind the super, well he'd have it. I pulled out my phone and furiously typed a message to Sebastian. For a moment, I considered deleting it, that dark voice in my head suggesting he was in cahoots with Rebecca.

I stared at the last message he sent and felt a comfortable numb set in. I pressed send. I had been the bigger person, but after last night, I didn't want to read anything from him. I flipped to his profile and blocked his number. I'd deal with that situation when I saw him next.

"First Damien, then Sebastian. Now we're playing by your rules." I stormed off toward my apartment to prepare for my next confrontation with the bigwig of Revelations.

"Mr. Smith," Damien stood with his back to the door, studying something on his desk. "I wasn't expecting you to return so soon."

I held the length of my tie, tightening it around my neck. I craned my neck as it brushed against the scruff under my chin. I tried not to scratch at my torso, annoyed at the layers of fabric rubbing against the hair on my stomach. I drew the front of my jacket close, fastening the buttons. Standing tall, I broadened my shoulders, my body groaning as I corrected my posture.

I held my tongue. If Damien wanted to play games, I'd humor him. In this chess match, I was prepared to go the distance. I rested my hands across my stomach. From this angle, Damien might be mistaken for an attractive man. He was wide in the shoulders, tapering down until the muscle reached his waist. I imagined he spent plenty of time in his home gym, developing those muscles. Vanity struck me as a pillar of his personality.

"Can I help you?" He didn't turn around.

"I'd appreciate a modicum of your attention."

His back straightened and his head turned enough I could make out the smile on his face. I fought to keep my hands from shaking, switching to holding them behind my back. The last time I demonstrated a backbone, I had been fired.

"A modicum, you say? Well, you have my attention, Mr. Smith. Are you going to make it worth my while?"

I had seen it from Sebastian, and even Rebecca, the cockiness that came with the employees of Revelations. I might look the part, or at least a low-budget version. The question on my mind right now, could I keep from hurling on the floor as I attempted to play the part?

Deep inhale. "Yes. At least enough that I've picked out my desk. Phillip is going to need to move to the shared workspace."

His eyes widened. Subtle. He managed to hold the rest of his face perfectly in place, but I had piqued his interest. He had turned to face me, finally, the entirety of his attention was now focused on me. I thought about reaching into my messenger bag and pulling out my portfolio, but this required him to believe I understood the ethos of Revelations.

"What is good and evil?"

"Am I being quizzed?" His head cocked to the side as his eyes narrowed.

"Do you answer questions with questions?" Alejandro's jaw would have dropped as I tried to imitate that suave personality that landed him a non-stop line of overnight guests.

"It's a societal construct, moving as the populace grows and evolves," he answered slowly.

"So, would you say the superheroes of Vanguard are good or evil?"

He started to speak and stopped. Leaning back against his desk, his pointer fingers tapped against the wood as he considered the question. Damien Vex studied me, trying to understand where I was going with this line of questioning. The smile had vanished, and I couldn't tell if he was amused with my new approach to requesting a job.

"Is a man good if he saves a babe from a burning building so he can be on the news?" I asked.

This was the longest conversation we had where he didn't hurl an insult. Either I was learning, or I had piqued his curiosity enough to satiate the bully in him.

I continued. "I think they do good things for society, but intent matters. Catering to their egos creates monsters that we call protectors."

I understood the goals of Revelations enough to predict his answer. I reached into my messenger bag and produced the black binder holding my newly designed spread. I started to hand it to him, but pulled back as his hand reached to receive it.

"Revelations stands between the light and dark, good and evil, right," I handed him the portfolio, "and wrong."

I held my breath, worried I had overplayed my hand. Had I built up my work too much? Was that actually the purpose of Revelations? I didn't know how Alejandro kept up the bravado all evening and not pass out behind the bar.

"Infamous Hearts?" Damien read. The words were accusatory. I had to rally, or he might not look any further.

"You wanted a look behind their heroics. As an avid comic book fan, I can promise you, your prime demographic will understand that every hero is defined by their heart."

He skimmed through the article, and I couldn't tell if he read the drivel. I wasn't a writer, nor would I ever claim to understand their job. It was enough to let the design speak on the page.

"You used genuine charcoal?"

"Yes, sir." I had made the chalky substance for college and thought there was no time like the present to break it out. I used burnt wood to grind into the page, sprinkling debris on the paper, tarnishing the white space. It covered the right margin of the page, where I had cut out a painting of liquid black and layered on top, a giant white figure made of light.

"You've essentially turned this fledgling hero into the villain. There is pure vitriol on the page, as if you had a grudge against this up-and-coming hero."

"I put my faith in the hero." I could feel my face flush as I shifted my weight from one foot to the other in hopes of alleviating the anxiety. "I know better now."

"Is this your best work?"

"Not even close," I admitted. Given a few days, I could have made it a showstopper. Right now, it was enough to impress another designer, but it hadn't reached the level I knew I was capable of achieving.

A warm tone filled the air. Our eyes remained locked in a showdown, chucking daggers at one another. The door behind me opened, and I held perfectly still. I must have barged in just before a scheduled meeting.

He walked up to me, to the point where our chests almost touched. He handed the portfolio to somebody behind me. "Thoughts?" He took a step back, waiting to hear the new couple's opinion of my work.

I could smell him before I turned. The cologne mingled with his scent enough that I blushed at the thought of him naked in bed. I wanted to turn around and slap him across the face. But even as the thought entered my head, guilt tugged at my heart.

"Introductions are in order," Damien started. "Sebastian, you know," I turned slightly, dreading the second name he was about to announce.

"Rebecca is the head of our marketing."

"We've met," I said. I expected her to be covered in bruises, perhaps missing a tooth from the sucker punch

Slipstream delivered. Either she walked away unscathed, or she had a miracle touch with make-up.

"It's..." She paused, putting on a performance where she dragged out the tension. I prepared to retaliate, to comment on her lack of style, or comment about her cry for attention with the bright red lipstick. "It's well thought out, contemporary, but has an edge to it. I don't know if all our sponsors would approve, but I can think of one or two that would be willing to advertise on an edgier spread."

Did Rebec—Wraith just compliment me? I expected her to tear me down and leave me the victim of another tongue lashing. But not only did she compliment me, she mentioned sponsors, which meant she saw a future for me in the company. Something was amiss, off, and for the life of me, I couldn't sort out the rules of this game she played.

"Sebastian?" Damien leaned to the side, looking past me to his art director. "Thoughts?"

I clenched my jaw, preparing to see Sebastian for the first time since he bailed on our date. In my head, I vilified him, holding firmly to the anger I had about him willing to sacrifice Vincent. I feared bumping into him and had fortified my heart for this situation.

He stared at me, but despite the calm facade, I could tell something weighed on his mind. Rebecca thrust my portfolio into his chest, forcing him to take a look. With a slight shake of his head, he started scanning the pages.

I held firm as he struggled to keep his jaw from opening. He gave a slight nod, not letting on that the superpowered person I shredded in the article was him. Rebecca knew, and by the growing smirk on her face, she was more than satisfied that the door between Sebastian and I had slammed shut.

"It's solid work."

"Come, Sebastian. I've never heard you short on criticism," Rebecca goaded him.

It dawned on me, Damien and I were the mundane humans in the room. Unless Sebastian had been ignoring his texts, he and Rebecca knew the other's identity. If a fight broke out, things would get messy. The owner's prodding didn't help Sebastian's demeanor.

"The article needs to be given to a journalist. As for the design work, it's innovative. It pushes the boundaries of what we'd permit in the book, and that's part of our trademark. I think we'd be foolish to let the Beacon's most talented designer slip through our fingers."

I was about to say thank you for the compliment, but he ruined it by adding the modifier. Rebecca had been terrorizing Beacon employees and now Sebastian mentioned poaching me from the magazine. All this time, I had thought they were valuing my work, but they had an ulterior motive. One piece at a time, they were attempting to dismantle the Beacon, and I had fallen victim to their twisted game.

"Welcome to the staff, Mr. Smith."

Damien extended his hand and out of politeness, I accepted. The pack of wolves had closed in and slaughtered their sacrificial lamb. I needed to get out of here and put space between me and whatever scheme I had stumbled into.

"You start tomorrow. For now, I need to speak with Rebecca and Sebastian about our largest sponsor to date."

And with that, I was dismissed.

───

I exited the elevator into the lobby. A single woman sat behind the counter of the oversized room. There were a few people milling around, eating lunch on a bench. I had been awarded a senior graphic design position, the very thing I'd been after for the last year. Yet, in my heart, the victory was hollow, and stung almost as much as failure.

"What have you gotten yourself into?"

I meandered through the lobby until I reached the revolving door. With a push, I stepped inside and exited into the courtyard, greeted by the late morning heat. It was either from the lack of clouds or the abundance of layers I wore, but the sweating started quickly. There was nothing more miserable than an overheated Griffin Smith.

I pulled off the jacket, loosened the tie, and unfastened the top button. It wasn't my usual self, but anything was better than feeling stuffy in my own skin.

"Now, do I celebrate with Alejandro, or do I commiserate with Xander? Bernard." I fished out my phone and texted Bernard, seeing if he'd be free for dinner later tonight. Korean tacos, cheap beer, and a healthy dose of sagely advice. I couldn't go wrong.

He cleared his throat as I pressed the send button.

"Griffin," the fortress I built for my critique had lowered just enough that hearing him say my name caused my heart to race. "What are you doing?"

I ground my jaw, forcing myself to relive the embarrassment the other night. I wasn't prepared for a one-on-one with Sebastian, but after showing me his true colors, I had enough fuel to keep myself on fire.

"What do you mean?" I turned to confront him. If there was any chance of my heart melting and throwing myself into his arms, it vanished at the sight of his furrowed brow and snarling lip.

"No warning? Nothing? You just threw together this little project without thinking I deserved a heads up? That stupid spread nearly exposed me."

"Oh, I didn't think you'd care. That must only happen when it serves you."

"You have no idea what I'm dealing with. Rebecca knows my secret. The crazy bitch would have killed you if I hadn't stepped in to save you."

I tried not to laugh, but failed. "You only stepped in

because I forced your hand. You'd have let her kill Vincent if I didn't throw myself into danger."

His eyebrows lowered and the tension in his jaw eased as his mouth gaped. "You played me? You manipulated me into exposing myself to the world?"

"Don't turn this around on me. You were going to let a man die." I stepped closer so he could hear my whisper. "I'm not the one wasting my abilities hiding. But then, I should know better. Being a hero and doing the right thing doesn't fit into your posh lifestyle."

He didn't have a reply. There was disappointment at the lack of a retort. One-by-one, I loaded the chamber, ready to pull the trigger should he push me. The old Griffin would have walked away and ugly cried while eating his feelings. That was before the Beacon fired me and a man I could have loved turned out to be just as much an asshole as all the others.

"It doesn't make it right." His words didn't have the same aggression as before. Had I struck a nerve and wounded the man? The confidence he normally exuded vanished, but I wouldn't let puppy dog eyes deter me.

"This isn't me." I held up the jacket and pointed to my tie. "Last night I got dressed up, I stepped outside my comfort zone. I waited for an hour. An hour, Sebastian. No texts. No calls. You didn't just bail, you ghosted me. And even after doing that, you didn't even say sorry."

"I'm—"

I held up my hand. "Don't. It's too little, too late. I might have my issues, but I don't deserve to be treated like garbage. Whatever is going on with you and Rebecca, that's between the two of you now. Be grateful I cared enough to tell you that Rebecca, that harpy, knows your secret."

"Griffin…"

I shook my head. This argument was over, this thing between us, it evaporated. I spun about and stormed off before he could see the tears welling in the corner of my eyes. He had already stabbed me in the heart. I wouldn't let him rob me of my dignity.

I had said my peace, but nothing about it felt good.

19

———————

"I'm okay."

"You don't look okay."

Bernard pulled a stool from under the table. Bottom's Up wasn't a busy place during the week, and other than Mick at the bar and a few patrons playing pool, it was dead. The narrow room had a bar on one side and tables lining the opposite wall. He could tell I had something on my mind when he gestured for us to sit at a table instead of our usual spot at the bar.

The Ward was a tight-knit community and after living here for years, it had become an extended family. By day we hopped from restaurants to the coffee shop, but once the sun went down, this dive bar transformed into the catch-all for gay men. It didn't hurt that the drinks were dirt cheap, and, with a little flirting, Mick might top you off without charging.

"To be honest, you look like you were hit with a truck."

Bernard had a knack for being direct without being judgmental. He didn't sugarcoat his words, and more often than not, his brand of tough love hit home.

He raised his glass, taking a swig of beer. His mustache had grown long enough that he had to wipe it after every drink. When I first met him, he had kept it trimmed, but as of late, he'd turned into a mountain man. While he was wonderful at solving the problems of others, he rarely shared his own demons. If he thought it was going unnoticed, he was sorely mistaken.

"Everybody knows I don't handle change well." I swirled the whisky in my glass until the smell reached my nose. "This has been a lot of change."

"Would you do it again?"

"Yes. No. Maybe? I honestly don't know." I took a sip, pacing myself so I didn't have a repeat of last night. "I'm tired of this, Bernard. I've been spinning my wheels for so long, and then these great opportunities come along, and..."

"They're not so great?"

"The Beacon treated me like dirt. Maybe I—"

"If you say you deserved it, I'll reach across this table and knock the stupid out of you."

Tough love.

"Apparently, all my career needed was for me to go morally bankrupt. Awesome Griffin, you're great at your job, but ethics are holding you back."

Bernard raised an eyebrow. I had barely explained the situation beyond leaving the Beacon and attempting a position at Revelations. Alejandro and Xander would have pressed for more details, but not Bernard. He knew when to push forward and give me a swift kick in the butt and when to let my omission of details stand.

"I think we've established how much I love superheroes."

"I just assumed you're wearing undies with a giant, 'pow' or 'bam' on them," he teased.

"So, you have x-ray vision now?"

He squinted as he put a finger on each temple. "Looks like I was wrong." He gave me a wink. "Impressive none the less."

Did I mention Bernard also had the ability to drop the levels of tension with a single statement? In the friends' department, I couldn't deny how lucky I was.

"The Beacon wasn't perfect, but we lifted up the heroes. Revelations, I basically dragged a new hero through the mud to make a good first impression."

"Ah, now I see."

"I got the job. They saw the value of my work. Hell, they even complimented my design. That was more than I ever got working at the Beacon."

"Which is a shame," he took another drink, wiping his mustache again. I wanted to reach across the table and cut the hairs from his lip. "I have a subscription. I've always enjoyed your work."

"Really?" I shouldn't be surprised that a superhero subscribed to the Beacon. He thought he was being stealthy, hiding his secret identity, but unless he had a twin saving the world from aliens, I knew the man behind Sentinel's mask.

"I signed up when you first got the job. I needed to see what all this hero obsession was about."

"Sure, you did."

"Okay, the men in leather didn't hurt."

Eventually we'd have *the* talk, but for now, I let Sentinel hide in his closet.

"I appreciate that. Revelations likes to kick the heroes in the gut. I feel like they're all about turning them into villains."

"So, a job that undervalues you, but has good ethics, or a job that values you and has bad ethics. I think you're the only person who can make that decision."

"You're not going to pick for me?"

He shook his head. "I can barely keep my life together. You don't want me making decisions for you."

If this wasn't difficult enough, there was something heavier weighing on me. The debate between good and bad reminded me of Sebastian. I wanted to ask Bernard what he thought, but I had already come dangerously close to revealing Sebastian's secret. I might have stormed off in a huff, but the more I dwelled on the situation, the more I feared I had made some incredibly dumb decisions.

Bernard finished his beer, hopped off his stool, taking the glass to the bar. He slowed as he walked back, pursing his lip in disapproval. Instead of returning to his seat, he wrapped his arms around me, squeezing. I had watched the man crush brick with his bare hands as he fought off the Sewer King's rat invasion. Right now, I needed those steely arms to remind me I wasn't alone.

"This isn't about the job, is it?"

"Sebastian—" I didn't know how to put it. "We'd barely started dating, and it got complicated. I think we're from two different worlds."

Bernard gave me one last squeeze before grabbing his stool and sitting next to me. I leaned my head on his shoulder, falling into my ongoing pit of misery.

"In your comics, do superheroes and supervillains fall in love?"

"Yeah, happens all the time." Over the years, just about every hero had fallen for a villain. It had become a cliché at this point, but somehow, they found a way to overlook their—

"I see what you did there."

"I'm not just a pretty face."

"I think I might have made a mistake." It was bad

enough that I lit the bridge on fire by including Sebastian into the spread for Revelations. But I decided to nuke it to smithereens when I read him the riot act. The anger about being stood up had melted away to worry. Had I misread the situation? Worse, had I overreacted out of fear?

"You really need to quit your day job and become a therapist."

Bernard laughed. "I do it for free. Besides, the day job has its perks."

I gave him a poke in the ribcage. Bernard Castle, the big burly man, giggled. The sound freed me from my spiral downward.

"Wearing leather *is* a perk, I guess." I couldn't resist. I didn't want to throw him out of his superhero closet, but I did want him to know he was seen. Besides, what's a deep dark secret for if not to bring people together? Okay, that's a bit too noble. I really just wanted to mess with him.

"Wait—What?"

The earbuds slide into place. With a couple of taps on my phone, the hundreds of playlists scroll across the screen. Oldies? Rock? Whiney men with guitars? Post new wave exper—really? I must have been trying to work through something when I made that one.

"For the lonely." Every song on the list had been

selected to tug at the heart strings and drag me through an emotional hell. When life knocked you to the ground, nothing like kicking yourself in the gut. At this point, I estimated less than ten songs in before the waterworks turned on and I cried myself to sleep.

Until then, I'd replay the events of the day until I dissected every possible outcome. Once I thought of a better scenario, I'd tap rewind and start over. This would go on until I had a dozen options of things I could have done better. If I spent this much time thinking before I ran my mouth, perhaps I'd be listening to something more upbeat.

"Griffin." I scooted to the edge of the couch. Leaning with my elbows on my knees, I fixated on the geometric pattern of the rug. Gray and brown squares intersected, and in the corner of one, a thread had pulled loose. Touching it with my toe, I debated hunting down a pair of scissors. "Griffin, you're hopeless."

I tapped the play button, and the sounds of the city grew distant. Impending heartache pushed its way through my walls, finding every crack and misfitting outlet cover. If that wasn't enough to induce a pity party, I eyed the painting.

The white paint had started as an attempt to erase the admiration. As it splattered against the canvas, I thought it might erase the stain Sebastian had left on my heart. When I massaged it into the painting, obscuring his features until he was unidentifiable, it did nothing to bandage the crumbling organ in my chest. The lack of satisfaction gave way to anger, and the plan had gone from hiding Sebastian to revealing the truth.

I walked over to the canvas, plopping myself into my chair. The man of pure white light looked more like a snowstorm gone horribly wrong. There were areas of the original painting poked through, bits of an arm and thigh, but everything produced a blinding light. To the casual viewer, it'd appear like a toddler's painting destined for the fridge. For a superhero lover, they'd see the Ward's newest hero... powered person. He might be many things, but hero was not one of them.

"Why are you so hung up on him?" I could feel my throat vibrate as I spoke, but with the earbuds in place, I couldn't hear my own voice. "You're talking to yourself again, Griff." It wasn't bad until I argued with myself.

It had only been a few days. Sebastian didn't deserve my breakup playlist, but he had been special. What if I had ruined an opportunity with *the* one? The heartache took hold and sank its hooks into my chest.

I poked at the cloths lying underneath my easel, seeing if any of them were remotely clean. I snatched the cleanest one and picked up a small can of turpentine. A few drops on the rag and I started carefully rubbing it along the surface of the painting. The white lifted, revealing the original painting.

"There you are," I whispered. Gentle, wide circles, a fast

brush along the face. The white faded a little at a time until I could see Sebastian's eyes. With a few more passes, his face peeked through the white, as if the light on his face had turned softer than the rest of his body.

The painting served as a symbol. The damage had been wrought, and no matter how careful I was, things wouldn't go back to the way they were. I wondered if there was turpentine for the heart? Maybe a little dabbed here and there and Sebastian and I could remain friendly.

A low beep broke through the music. One of the apps on my phone wanted attention, but I couldn't stop staring at a pipe dream. The white had receded enough to see his chest, his *beautiful* chest. I hadn't gotten my fill of it before I blew up. I'm sure if I thought back to all my failed relationships, this would win the award for the fastest ending.

"Great, Griffin," I scoffed, "you found something you're good at."

The beep sounded three times in rapid fire. I recognized this one. The HeroApp™ wanted my attention. Something big must be happening in the vicinity. I reach to my pocket, and it sounded one more time.

"I get it already," I growled.

I fished it out to see the alert flashing. Somewhere a villain was doing who knows what. With a click, I could see the name in the top corner with a black profile icon.

"Wraith," I cursed.

The radius of the alert had me right on the edge of the

area labelled, "Be Alert." I scrolled through the map to see where she decided to strike. Two blocks away, the bitch of darkness was terrorizing—

"The Beacon?"

Unlike before, the alert already noted a body count. She had gone from terrifying Beacon employees to killing. If this was going to be her swan song, she'd be out to do as much damage as possible. If the heroes of the Ward weren't quick, she'd leave a trail of bodies leading right into the lobby of the building.

The phone shook, and the radius expanded. I had never seen it do that before. In the lower right-hand corner, a picture of Zipper appeared, followed by a red X. The fastest man alive wasn't a match for a woman capable of robbing him of his sight. Hopefully that meant Cobalt was—

"Holy shit." Cobalt's image and another red X.

Her body count reached double digits. It might be okay, as the app didn't differentiate between dead and unconscious. But knowing how close she came to killing Sofia, I feared Rebecca had finally moved firmly into the villain column. Stopping her now required a prison cell or death.

Outside, the sky started to brighten as if the sun were rising off in the distance. I glanced at the phone again as the body count continued to climb. Moving closer to the window, I nearly had to squint. It wasn't coming from the horizon. Somewhere between the buildings, a brilliant white illuminated the street.

A blinding light flew between the buildings.

Rubbing my eyes, I tried to shake the multicolored orbs. This had happened before. Except last time it had been... Sebastian. The gasp was loud enough to be heard over the music.

"He's heroing."

20

I HAD NEVER PUT ON MY SNEAKERS SO QUICKLY. I DIDN'T bother locking the door as I sped toward the elevator. Rapidly pushing the button didn't make the doors open any faster. I threw open the metal door to the stairwell and started down the three flights.

By the time I reached the bottom, my lungs struggled. My pulse thumped through my veins as I hit the door and spilled into the hallway. I nearly tripped over a wrinkle in the old carpet.

"How rude," came a shrill voice.

"Sorry, Ms. McNamara," I panted. I gave her a slight salute before continuing to speed down the hallway. There was no point in telling her I was on my way to make sure a superhero crushed a villain.

Once I hit the street, I raised the phone, ensuring the

fight hadn't changed location. A quick glance at the bottom corner ensured that Sebastian hadn't already been knocked out of the fight. I started to jog, leaning forward, forcing my legs to pump.

I don't know why I was in a hurry. It wasn't like I was going to show up and save the day. If two of the Ward's heroes were already dispatched, Wraith would most likely kill me on sight. But part of me needed to be there, to witness Sebastian transforming into a hero.

But what if he wasn't? What if Rebecca had gotten to him and this was his first outing at becoming something dark and twisted like her? My legs burned as I pushed harder. No, that little voice of doubt needed to sit down and shut up. Sebastian might have taken the long way around, but I believed in him.

My pacing slowed as people fled the next block. Men and women dragged their children away from the fight. In a city where something like this happened every other day, we had grown numb to the constant attacks. To see a man holding a little girl as he dragged his wife away from the origin meant it was bad.

"You're going the wrong way," yelled a woman.

"She's killing everybody," screamed her partner.

I ignored their warnings. Was he attempting to save the city? And after our fight? I had to be by his side. After the tongue lashing I delivered, I would have thought he'd cement his desire to hide amongst the mundane citizens. It was like the comic books.

I had faith that Sebastian was making a stand.

I sidestepped a car door as it swung open. A man popped his head out, confused by the rush of people fleeing the danger zone. I turned slightly, pointing in the direction of safety. "Supervillain, go that way."

"But you're—"

I couldn't hear him as he argued my logic. I rounded the corner onto the block with the Beacon. Leaning against a lamppost, I huffed and puffed, trying to catch my breath. I hadn't run that far in years. If I dropped dead now, I wouldn't be able to perform my sidekick duties.

If Sebastian was attempting to be a hero, I owed it to him to be present. But if I was wrong, and he was in league with Rebecca, I might be the only person able to sway the tide. With this many people screaming bloody murder, it might be the first villain alert to catch the attention of the Centurions.

The building that housed the Beacon stood halfway down this block, or at least it should. A wall of black ten stories tall had radiated outward, swallowing the middle of the block. It extended across the street, consuming nearby buildings. I could see why people were running. This wasn't a supervillain stealing money from an ATM. Wraith had laid claim to a piece of the city and who knew what she was doing inside the gloom.

With a steadying breath, I started a light trot toward the wall of black. I had no idea what to expect inside, but the knot in my stomach told me things would never be the same again.

I slowed as I caught the sight of a cape flapping in the breeze. The blue and silver clad man laid on his back, unmoving. What would a hero do? Charge into the unknown or make sure the victims were safe? I never thought comic books would be the backbone of my morality.

I dropped next to Cobalt, leaning close to his nose. He was barely breathing.

I tapped Cobalt's face, trying to wake him. His leg was bent in an unnatural position. Blood coated his uniform and had torn away from one of his shoulders. The man had taken a beating, and despite that, he refused to die.

I crawled on my hands and knees to Zipper. "This is going to hurt," I prepared the man. He groaned loudly as I rolled him onto his back, looking for any broken limbs. His nose was broken and one of his eyes had swollen shut.

"You're alive," I said. "You'll make it." The words were more for me than for him. Two of the Ward's bravest were down for the count, and now everything depended on a rookie hero and his mundane sidekick.

I pulled out my phone and stared at the giant blinking alert telling me to flee. I swiped past and scrolled through my contacts. With a click, the phone started ringing.

"Griffin, what's—"

"Wraith has taken out Zipper and Cobalt," I told Bernard.

"I'm sure it'll be okay."

"I need a Centurion."

"Most of them are in another dimension right now."

"I didn't say *the* Centurions. I need one."

After our last conversation, he might think I suspected him of being one of the premiere superheroes on Earth. The Centurions were the protectors of the planet and rarely dealt with street level crime, but I needed to call in a favor. It wasn't time to be coy. Sorry Bernard, but I couldn't avoid your secret any longer.

"I don't—"

"I need Sentinel."

The phone went silent. Zipper groaned and then coughed, blood spitting from his lip. Even if he and Cobalt woke up, they weren't in any shape to fight.

"I'm clearing the mission with operations."

"Track my phone."

"Griffin, stay safe."

That wasn't an option.

21

Liquid black. The wall resembled paint on my palette, and if I reached out, I'd find it smeared against my palms. Wraith wielded the black like a weapon, the tendrils emerging and attacking at her command. I half expected them to shoot out and drag me in.

Something on the other side of the wall exploded. A car? The sound of crushing brick followed. Was Sebastian inside already duking it out with Wraith? Had she claimed the lives of the Beacon employees, or was she torturing before murdering them?

I pushed my hand against the black, surprised at the goop. Unlike before, her shadows had substance, like a wall of gelatin. My hand easily sank in, and I retracted it at the sound of sheering metal.

"Thirty paces forward, twenty to the left." I tried to

guesstimate the distance to the Beacon. If this was like the previous attack, I'd be going in blind and without my sight, there wasn't much I could do to help Sebastian. But if I could help protect the Beacon employees while he concentrated on dispatching Wraith...

"In for a penny..."

I stepped into the darkness.

"In for a pound."

I cracked open my eyes to find nothing changed. Open or closed, the world remained black. It was darker than any night I had ever experienced, and no matter where I turned, it felt like an infinity. I was officially in Wraith's world and at any moment, I expected to feel her hands grip my neck.

I started counting. Each step meant further from safety. Even if I turned around and bolted, I couldn't be sure I wouldn't run into a wall. I kept my hands in front of me, fearful I might stumble onto the soft skin of a killer.

Every muscle tensed as my palms pressed against an unknown object. Hard, cold, possibly metal, but otherwise, I couldn't identify the thing blocking my path. I turned to the left, taking steps closer to the building as I let my fingers trail on along the *thing.* They passed over a gap before touching something less smooth. An upside-down car had been flung onto the sidewalk.

Ten paces closer to the building, I had at least another fifty before I reached the area with glass doors leading inside the Beacon. Did Wraith's abilities penetrate walls? Did the darkness extend inside the building, or would it spill inside as I opened the door?

I reached the end of the car when something in the distance disrupted the veil of darkness. A burst of light shone through the darkness. My heart jumped, trying to shove its way into my throat. A second later, a brilliant figure vanished into the darkness. He blinked again in a furious flash of white, reminding me of late evening thunderstorms. Darkness, and then a brief bolt of lightning cutting through the veil of night.

Did he always know he could fly or was this a newly acquired ability? Beams of light shot from his palms, slicing through the black. Any belief that he might be in cahoots with Rebecca vanished. Black tendrils snaked around his body and each time they took hold, the light surged.

"He's fighting."

Sebastian could deal with Wraith. His sidekick would secure her targets. Comic books had prepared me for this moment. All those countless hours reading about the secret lives of heroes would finally pay off.

The light vanished again, and I shimmied along the sidewalk until I thought I was nearing the doors of the Beacon. I walked toward the building and nearly banged my head into a cement pillar. Every building felt the same, brick, maybe glass, but there was little to tell them apart. I moved along until my hands found a large shape protruding from the brick.

"The Beacon," I whispered. Every day for years, I had seen the sign on the side of the building. I hated the font they used, a tacky afterthought that no designer would have ever allowed. I was only ten feet from the entrance.

"You can't hide from me," boomed Wraith's voice. I shimmied quicker, worried she had discovered that I had entered her domain.

I found the handle of the door. Pulling at it, I stepped from the sidewalk into the Beacon. I stumbled over the threshold and as I caught my balance, I stood half covered in Wraith's black. With another step, I was standing in the lobby, free of her influence.

"Griffin?" Sofia had backed herself against the wall of the lobby. Her arm had been put in a sling. "She's back."

I nodded. Twice in as many days Sofia had endured Wraith's villainy. I didn't have time to go into a long explanation. If Sebastian kept her busy, I could at least help get the employees out of the rear exit.

"She's here for the Beacon." I pulled free of the darkness, surprised at the dryness on my skin. "She's been targeting employees."

"Why?"

That was a complicated question, and if I gave away too much information, it might lead back to Rebecca. Once Revelations was under suspicion, it'd put Sebastian in jeopardy. I had made that mistake once. If he could be a hero, I could be a sidekick.

"A magazine that publishes information about heroes? She probably thinks you know their identities or something." It wouldn't be the first time the Beacon had been attacked. The DataMiner constantly hacked the computers searching for information on the heroes they interviewed.

"What do we do?"

"Can't go out that way. We could stumble over her and wouldn't know it until she strangled us."

"Sir Unemployed," I recognized Janet's voice before she jumped down the last few stairs. Under other circumstances, I'd have gladly returned the insult. "Half the building is covered."

"Rear exit." I gave Sofia a slight shove to push her past the stairwell. I paused, making a grand gesture for Janet to follow. "After you, Lady Pain in the Ass."

"Griffin? What the hell are you doing here?"

My back straightened and fists clenched at the sound of Vincent's barking. He quickly worked his way down the stairs and I as he reached the last step, I debated driving my knuckles into his face.

"She's—"

"Yeah, yeah," I grumbled, "Wraith is here again. You're late for the party as usual. Is there anybody else upstairs?"

"Upstairs? No, everybody else got out." Vincent had a tell, his eyes cast downward when he was up to no good. He had been a horrible boss, and even now, he'd sacrifice anybody to protect his own life. Vincent wore his cowardice like a badge of honor.

"Follow Janet." I gave him a shove. There was nothing friendly about it, but unlike him, I'd rise above my dislike.

We crossed the lobby to a fire door that led down a hall to the rear entrance where the employees smoked. The darkness had expanded, starting to push further into the building. If she was capable of extending her influence, did that mean she had defeated Sebastian?

"Worry, later," I whispered.

We worked down the corridor until it turned left, a straight shot to the rear parking lot. I ran into a stopped Vincent. I was about to shove him forward when I noticed Sofia and Janet inching their way back.

"The hallway is blocked," Sofia said.

The darkness had worked its way through the walls, separating us from safety. Did Wraith have the ability to move through the darkness or did she still have to use a door like everybody else? The stupid app didn't have the necessary details to determine if my next actions were dumb.

"Grab my hands," I stepped around them, putting both hands behind me. "We're going through."

"No way in hell," Vincent argued. "She tried to kill me once already."

"You're not the only one, you idiot," Janet shot back. When this was over, I'd owe her a drink.

The man was a wretched boss, a horrible human. He didn't deserve my good graces or Janet's tempered reply. For hundreds of staff meetings, he gloated about how amazing he was. He prided himself on his managerial skills, but we all knew that was code for being a corporate thief. Because of him, I had lost my job. The anger radiated through my veins, reaching my hands as I balled my fists.

"You think you know what you're doing? You don't even—"

I grabbed him by the shirt with one hand and pressed my forearm against his throat with the other. I pinned him to the wall. This man had continued to demean me, chipping away at my confidence one remark at a time. I applied pressure, making it difficult for him to breathe.

His eyes remained wide as he slapped at my shoulder, trying to push me away. His lips sputtered, and I found myself wanting to see him collapse from the lack of oxygen. The bully couldn't defend himself, and I relished in the change of power between us. I recalled Sebastian's willingness to let him die, and it finally dawned on me; not all walk a righteous path, but it doesn't make them any less of a hero.

"You're not worth the trouble," I hissed.

I stepped back, letting go of the jerk. He doubled over, sucking in air as if he deserved it. At that moment, I empathized with Sebastian and the regret came rushing in. I'd have plenty of apologizes to make once I got them to safety.

"I don't even have an insult," Janet said. It was the best compliment I could receive from the woman. Her eyes darted from Vincent to me, and the edge of her lip turned upward.

"Screw that," Sofia said, "you're my hero."

I held out my hands. The moment they grabbed on, I dragged them forward, storming into the darkness. The same soupy sensation coated my skin. I had to remember to breathe, that the darkness wouldn't drown me.

Both women gripped my hands tightly. I made sure to return the squeeze, trying to comfort them through the black. Every so many feet I paused, kicking to the side to count the doors we passed. Four down, one more to go before we reached the tiny vestibule that would hold the door to freedom.

The light struck my face, and I pulled them out of the shadows. Before I could open my mouth, I saw another hand reach out of the shadows. Vincent emerged. The moment he spotted the door, he pushed past and ran toward the parking lot.

"Such a Goddamned coward." Sofia barked.

I held the door open, gesturing for them to escape. "Go, run and don't look back."

"You're not coming with us?"

"I have one more person to save."

Sofia gave a nod and exited. It was Janet who lingered, and I could tell she was chewing through a long list of insults. I'd have been shocked if she didn't get in one last jab as I threw myself into danger.

"You were always too good for the Beacon."

She bolted, catching up to Sofia. Wrapping her arm around the younger woman's waist, they jogged toward safety. I should have followed them and leave the super-hero antics to the people with powers, but I owed it to Sebastian. Janet's words struck a nerve, and I couldn't help but stare back down the hallway, rejuvenated and ready to end this fight.

"A compliment, Janet? Really?"

Okay, consider me shocked.

22

Her powers were growing. The entire building had been thrust into a perpetual night. I tried to recall how far down the corridor before the hall turned. I inched forward until my hand brushed the wall. Ninety-degrees to the right, I continued until I smashed into the door.

"How the hell am I going to help Sebastian?" My hand rested on the bar that'd open the fire exit into the lobby. It would be the perfect spot for Wraith to pull the door open, her eyes lighting up the empty space before she grabbed me. Gently, I pushed the door open and waited for certain doom.

"Too many movies, man." I only half believed the words as I whispered them.

Something slammed into the building, causing the walls to vibrate. In the lobby, a flash of light filled the space.

I couldn't be certain, but I swore I saw a man leap from the ground, soaring straight upward. Was he the one hammering away at the building, or was it Wraith?

I made my way toward the street. In a few feet, I'd be outside the door and at least then I'd be able to spot Sebastian within Wraith's muck. I balled my fists, as if I might be able to single-handedly take down a supervillain.

The breeze flowed through the lobby. Whatever had crashed into the building had shattered windows and the glass cracked under foot. I reached the door, careful to avoid the shards. Outside, the wind whipped at my shirt.

Without my eyes to guide me, I relied on my other senses. Smell? The city smelled nasty once you concentrated on it. Hearing? No screaming, just the howl of Mother Nature working her way between the buildings. Touch? Ew, the darkness already clung to my skin, and I didn't want to focus on that. Taste? Yeah, no, tasting Wraith was not on my priority list.

"I am the worst sidekick."

The hair on my arms stood on end a second before something plowed straight downward out in the street. It sounded as if a bomb had gone off, rocks spitting into the air in every direction. Broken asphalt assaulted my nostrils, and I imagined Wraith buried in a hole in the ground, put there by the Ward's newest hero. As for taste, still ew, and now I had a mouth full of dust.

"Is that all you've got?" Her voice came out of nowhere,

directionless and omnipotent. I suspected that she did it for a tactical advantage, but knowing Rebecca, she loved the idea of being a goddess.

Beams of light cut through the darkness, slamming into a shadowy figure. Sebastian hovered five stories above, both of his hands gripped together as his skin radiated a brilliant and beautiful glow. Could he see me? I wanted to cheer him on, to tell him I had been wrong.

Wraith constructed a shield of shadows. It cracked and shattered as if made from a solid substance. She pulled at the darkness, moving to her feet, using them to push against his light.

Heroes *could* exist in the gradient between black and white. The smile stretched across my face and I gave him a silent woot for support. When the adrenaline stopped pumping through my veins, I'd look back at the stupid mistakes and sort out which had been in the heat of the moment.

Her sphere of darkness wavered, letting the light of day wash over her domain. I covered my eyes, careful not to look away. I wanted to see the very moment he defeated that bitch. Her plan crumbled and the employees of the Beacon had gotten to safety. Whatever her motivation, Wraith was about to lose.

She grunted loud enough I could make out the swearing from across the street. But she wasn't the only one moaning. A few feet away, sprawled on the ground, Slipstream rolled over, clutching her side. The woman had joined the fight and, just like the other heroes, Wraith had bested the heroine.

I ducked low and worked my way over to her. My side-kick duties weren't limited to one hero. If I could help, I would. I dropped to my knees, shielded by an overturned car.

"We need to get you out of here." I was terrified to pull her hand from the wound. The blood was pouring freely and already leaving a puddle on the ground.

"He can't beat her." Her voice didn't match the bold black and white contrast of her uniform. The shard of glass sticking out of her torso was at least three inches long. It vanished between her hands and buried itself in her gut. If I had my phone, I'd call Xander, he'd know what to do.

"You're in no shape to fight," I whispered. "If you don't get that looked at soon…"

It was the dark reality of being a superhero. The normal folk had grown desensitized to the danger of living in a world with these titans. Hell, even I considered them like comic book characters. But in truth, every time a villain decided to unleash their wrath, we were only a misstep from death. Slipstream understood that, it's probably why she put on the uniform.

"I need to help him." She pulled her hands from the wound, trying to place them on the ground. Her eyes rolled back in her head as she hissed through clenched teeth.

Whether she liked it or not, she wasn't getting back into this fight.

"Can you teleport to the hospital?"

"Too," she gasped, "much pain."

"We need to slow the bleeding. You're going to be fine." I tried to sell the lie as I tore off my shirt. My last first aid class had been in high school, and I spent more time lusting after the teacher than I did paying attention.

"I'm going to pull the glass out." It was a bad idea. Every TV show said don't do it, but I couldn't pack the wound without moving the glass around shredding her insides. I had two bad options before me.

"It's going to—"

"Do it," she hissed.

Wadding up my t-shirt, I prepared to make the exchange. Deadly shard of glass for the absorbent material. Holding the end of the glass, I carefully pulled. The first attempt had my hands sliding along the crimson surface. Using my sleeve, I gripped the glass and gently pulled it free. It didn't matter how much care I took, Slipstream growled, whimpering between breaths.

I tossed the glass to the side and pushed the balled-up shirt against the cut. The blood continued to flow, and I couldn't understand how one human contained so much liquid. Or had; every time I thought about it, my stomach grew tighter. If we didn't move, she was going to die on the side of the street.

"Hold it in place," I got to my feet. "Up with me." I put my arms under her armpits and lifted her to her feet. Thankfully, the hero weighed almost nothing. Putting her arm over my shoulder, I wrapped the other around her waist, prepared to drag her along as we made our way to an ambulance, or cop car, anybody. Somebody.

Slipstream couldn't die. Not after she saved me and, now Sebastian. I wouldn't let it happen. If I had to make a deal with the devil himself, this wouldn't be how she died.

I nearly jumped out of my skin when a nearby upside down car screeched. The alarm whooped, echoing through the empty street. The white of Wraith's eyes turned in our direction.

There was nowhere to run, at least not that a supervillain couldn't easily reach. We'd be safe as long as Sebastian could—

The black poured out of her legs, running along the ground as if a dam had exploded. Her entire body grew, the shadowy figure owning the name Wraith. The liquid reached the sidewalk and moved over the curb as if it were alive.

The shield she created to stop Sebastian's bursts of light shot forward. Tendrils of black sped through the air, wrapping around him. Up to this point, she had been toying with her nemesis, and now it appeared as if she were done playing. Even as Sebastian attempted to blast away the shadows, they reformed until they gripped his limbs.

He punched at Wraith's otherworldly ability. When that didn't work, he attempted to fly out of reach, but they refused to let go. Sebastian locked eyes with me. I stood at the crossroads of an impossible decision. No matter what I did, the heroes of the Ward were about to die.

23

AN IMPOSSIBLE DECISION REQUIRES AN IMPOSSIBLE ANSWER. I lowered Slipstream to the ground, pressing her hands over my blood-soaked t-shirt. There was no plan, just a gut feeling that I needed to follow.

"You can't stop her," she whispered.

"I know," I said. But I could buy them time.

"Wraith!" I shouted as I turned back to the hulking mass of shadows. I approached the edge of the sidewalk, where her shadows licked at the concrete. Years of reading comic books had come to this.

"Pick on somebody your own size." Okay, my dialogue needed work, but right now I was too concerned with not peeing my pants. Her eyes were sinister on their own, but as she smiled, revealing pearly white teeth, she reminded me of the scary things children believe hid under their beds.

"You've won," I yelled, "you've beaten every hero in the Ward, so what? They were never your target."

"They never stood a chance." Her raspy voice held an air of arrogance, a trademark for villains. I doubted I could get her into a monologue, but if she wanted to hurt Sebastian, it wouldn't be by crushing his body.

"Great, you defeated them. You broke their bones, but they'll heal. You'll do this all over again."

"Or I could kill them."

"It's a onetime pain."

I took a step onto the street, my foot sinking into the muck. I expected her to swallow me in an instant, perhaps hurl me against the building like she had Slipstream. But my dull, boring, ordinary self had caught her off guard.

"Leave them." I took a deep breath, terrified of the next words out of my mouth. "Take me."

"Foolish," she spat, "so incredibly foolish."

The liquid rushed around my legs, squeezing until I feared she'd break my bones. She moved closer, gliding as she formed a sword like shape in her right hand. I wouldn't stand a chance, and no amount of begging or pleading would slow her. I prayed it gave Sebastian a chance to break free.

"Your boyfriend can't save you." She let loose a laugh

that sent a shiver down my spine. Off in the distance, her shadows drove Sebastian downward, slamming him into the ground hard enough to create a crater. The shock knocked cars back and shattered the windows in nearby buildings.

"I grow tired of playing with him."

I tried to bolt, to run in his direction, but she had encased my legs in the sludge. No matter how hard I pulled, my legs refused to move. She had gotten close enough I could feel her breath along my cheek. While she violated my personal space, she never let the sword leave my line of sight.

My desire to be a hero wavered. Tears flowed down my face. It wasn't Wraith who laughed at my fear, it was Rebecca. I wouldn't get another brunch with the guys. I wouldn't see my work on the front page of the magazine. As the future I wouldn't experience flashed before my eyes, one thing continued replaying. I wouldn't get the opportunity to apologize for the horrible things I said to Sebastian.

"You thought you could save them. *Him.* I might have broken every bone in his body, but you're the one who broke him. You—" She pressed dangerously close, well within striking distance.

I swiped with my arm, nails scraping along the woman's face. The black covered my hands, but for a split second, I could see the alabaster skin and four streaks of red. I tried for a second swing, but a shadow caught my arm.

"Die."

I expected the plunging of the sword, cracking my sternum and piercing my heart. I prepared for the impact, the pain, and transition from agony to the cold of death. But as I shut my eyes, it felt more like a hug around my waist and a quirk jerking motion.

I slammed into something, trying to cradle my head to prevent a concussion. I came to a stop, opening my eyes, prepared to make a dash for Sebastian. I wasn't on the street. Somehow, I had been yanked from harm's way and dropped on... the Beacon roof?

I spun about and saw Slipstream, still covering her wound. Her suit hid the severity, but the pale features and circles under her eyes didn't lie. She had risked certain death to save me.

"You're a hero," I said. I took a step forward, determined to be by her side until help came or... The tears didn't stop streaming down my face. I had never been this close to heroes, and as she put her life on the line to save me, I found it much more real than comic books had let on.

"We are," she winked. In a puff of smoke, she vanished.

"No!"

I ran to the edge of the roof, looking over the waist-high wall to see Slipstream teleport behind Wraith. Bringing down bloody fists, she stuck the villain across the neck. Before the tendrils could ensnare her, she teleported away.

I let out a breath, thankful she escaped.

"No!" I shouted, as she blinked in again. She could

barely hold herself upright, but she refused to quit. This time, however, she didn't blink away. "No. No. No."

There were no speeches, no maniacal laughter. Wraith plunged the sword into the hero's torso. The black pushed out the back of her suit, holding the poor hero in the air. I held out hope until Slipstream's body went limp.

Wraith pulled the sword free, letting it merge with the rest of her body. She could have gone after Sebastian finished him off, but I had made her an offer she couldn't refuse. Pointing in my direction, she wanted me to shake in terror before she claimed her prize.

I had run out of terror. The only emotion pumping through my body was rage. The chances of me surviving against Wraith were non-existent, but I wasn't going to go down without a fight.

Running to the stairwell leading into the building, I grabbed the push broom we used to prop the door open. It'd be locked from the inside, a fact I learned the hard way the first time I decided to take my lunch break on the sunshine covered rooftop. With a quick spin, the broom fell off, and I had a weapon, not a good one, but it was better than trying to cut her with my wit.

The shadows crept along the ledge before she appeared. Preparing for the swing, I charged toward her stain. She crawled over the wall like a monster from a child's worst nightmares. I screamed as I swung. It landed on the side of her head, bursting into splinters. Despite the force of the blow breaking the stick on her skull, Wraith didn't flinch.

"Cute."

I backed away, eyeing the sharpened pole. If she got close enough, I could stab her. If I hit a fleshy spot, maybe that'd wound her enough to get away. No, I wasn't going to wound her. If this came down to me or her, it was time to admit playing nice wasn't an option.

I thrust the sharp end of the broom stick toward her throat. Wraith slithered to the side, batting it away with her arm as if it were a mild inconvenience. She moved forward, unthreatened by my determination.

"Griffin Smith, did you just try to kill me?"

"Try?" I thrust again. She moved with speed and grace, pushing my arm out wide with one hand while the other grabbed my throat. For a moment, she held still, and I thought she'd drag out this game of cat and mouse.

"You're less than pathetic." Her fingers tightened, and she lifted me upward until my toes barely touched the roof.

The black peeled away from her face, neck and chest. She was no longer Wraith, a creature born from the shadows. Rebecca snarled, almost as vile as her alter-ego. I shouldn't be surprised to see the full face of make-up, carefully applied with a practiced hand. Being beautiful didn't make her any less evil.

"Who," I dropped the broom stick, holding her wrist to

give myself the ability to breathe. "Who gave you the black eye?"

Into the air and with more force than should be possible, she slammed me onto the ground. The world shook, blackened, and for a second I couldn't tell which way was up. I kicked, trying to put distance between me and the villain.

"Killing you will be so gratifying." The black oozed along her skin until Rebecca vanished, swallowed by Wraith.

I was about to die.

***

I imagined death as falling down a hole, the light growing distant until it snuffed out. I expected it to hurt for at least a second. After that would come the ever after. Peace? Hell? I hadn't given it much thought up to this point.

I didn't expect death to envelope me in a searing light.

My hand brushed against the broomstick, anchoring me. I remained on the roof. This wasn't death, it was...

"Sebastian," I gasped.

Narrowing my eyes, I could see Wraith's black form blotting out the blaze. Behind her, an angelic being made of pure light hovered in the air. I couldn't make out his features, but those broad shoulders were impossible to disguise.

"Haven't had enough?" Wraith's confidence didn't falter. Her body count continued to climb. She had defeated him once before, and now it was tying up loose ends. At this rate, she'd be promoted to a top tier villain and the Centurions might finally intercede.

Wraith's feet hovered above the roof, defying gravity as she waited for Sebastian to make his move. He moved around her, gliding effortlessly until he stood between me and the villain. I commended him on protecting me, but I feared just as much for *his* safety.

"He's not part of this, Rebecca."

Villain psychology 101, trying to connect to the part of them that might still be good. For any other villain it might have worked, but I suspected that the only good bone in her belonged to unlucky bedfellow.

"They're all part of it. This infernal magazine will perish one way or another."

"You don't have to—"

By the time she swung her hand toward his neck, it had extended into her signature blade. He stepped back, far enough out of reach that she hadn't left a scratch. Wraith's other hand extended and now she swung in an intricate pattern, moving closer, pressing him back until Sebastian nearly tripped over my legs.

"I hope he was worth dying for."

The words came out in a low hiss, as if she were part snake. I realized that Sebastian hadn't made a move to attack Wraith. He ducked out of the way, stepped to the side, and maneuvered as if he had become an expert on missing the edges of her mystic blades. Sebastian hadn't been entirely honest. I suspected that, if I started digging, there might be a paper trail of luminary superhero sightings.

His fingers tightened while ducking under a swipe that would have left him headless. Shooting upright, he hooked his knuckles under her chin. Wraith did a backward somersault in the air, spinning twice before she smashed onto the roof. I nearly cheered for my burly protector.

He turned to me. "Are you alright?"

Something about his voice was different, almost breathy. While his voice might have grown increasingly calm, it was the only thing I noticed that had changed. His upper body dimmed to the point where I could make out his larger features. Right now, I wanted to rush to the man and shower him in kisses. Not only had he stood up for the right thing, he had done it without compromising his ethics.

"You saved me?"

I couldn't make out the facial expression, but I imagined that he grinned at the question. Instead, his body slumped slightly, exhausted. The man staggered, and I held out my arms as if I might be able to slow the descent of his hulking frame. At the last moment, he caught himself.

"I'm running on empty," he admitted.

"You saved the Ward."

He turned down his abilities, not enough to reveal his lack of clothing, but enough that I could make out the silhouette of his face. I didn't hesitate as I grabbed the side of his head and pressed my lips against his mouth. I was surprised at the lack of warmth coming from the light he produced. He stiffened before relaxing, putting an arm around my waist.

My hand travelled up his ribcage until he grunted and pulled away. Without seeing the black and blue along his skin, it was impossible to tell his condition.

"Are *you* okay?" I asked.

He rested an arm on my shoulder, less for intimacy and more for support. After the last hour of trading blows with Wraith, I was surprised he had rallied.

"I've had better days." He leaned in and gave me a peck. "Doing better now."

"I need to apologize. I didn't—"

"You were being a good sidekick."

"I don't know about that." Was our fight a necessary process for his journey to becoming a hero? I hadn't thought about it in that context.

"I can be a hero." His voice was soft. Even with the ability to fly and hurl vehicles, he found a way to be vulnerable. "I can be the hero you deserve."

"Sebastian..." My heart ached in a way it hadn't in ages. I wanted countless nights of cuddling on the couch while reading comics with this man. He was the part of my life I had been missing, the piece that offered healing I hadn't thought possible.

Sebastian's back arched. The light dimmed enough to make out the contorted silent howl on his face. On the left side of his torso, I watched as the sliver of black poked through his flesh. We had made the rookie mistake of believing Wraith lie defeated on the rooftop.

"No!" I shouted. I tried to pull at his body, to jerk him from Wraith's clutches.

She lifted him into the air, his body sliding further down the blade. I gripped the broomstick. She shook him free, hurling Sebastian's limp body toward the stairwell door. Before she could turn her attention on me, I thrust the tip of the broomstick into her chest.

Wraith screamed.

It wasn't as gruesome or impressive as her blade, but the shadows fled the spot where the wood buried into her chest. I shoved harder. The black ooze that normally coated her skin flailed, retreating, leaving bits of naked flesh exposed.

"Defeated by a pathetic man," I hissed. Leaning forward, I braced my feet and pushed as hard as possible. I couldn't tell if it sank any further, but her screams were satisfaction enough. Wraith staggered, and I thought I might be able to shove her off the roof. I knew she could fly, but hopefully that required concentration.

Her screams stopped. Whatever pain I had caused didn't last. It wasn't over. Rebecca vanished, and the Ward's most dangerous villain prepared to claim another victim. Her hands stretched until the fingers turned into lengthy talons.

"Not by you."

The burst of light struck Wraith, sending her flying from the roof. I thought Sebastian mustered another laser beam, but this one was bigger. I caught sight of the human bathed in a white brilliance, holding her by the neck as they soared over the street. Despite the choke-hold, she clawed at him, never showing signs of surrender.

I ran toward the ledge. Sebastian's body went super nova, followed by a boom that sounded like a bomb going off. The ripples that followed shattered the glass along dozens of buildings, shaking the very concrete under my feet. Car alarms down the street sounded, filling the dead air.

I rubbed my eyes, blinking rapidly in hopes to regain my sight. Squinting, I scoured the area below, barely able to make out the vehicles. The evidence of their fight could be seen up and down the street, but neither Sebastian nor Wraith were anywhere to be found.

"He sacrificed himself," I whispered.

I had been furious with the man before today, and that quickly dissolved. Surely, as he defeated Wraith, he sped away to conceal his identity. Even as I tried to rationalize his absence, the doom crept in.

Without any evidence of his survival, my greatest fears festered, sinking their talons into my back. In comic books, death was a plot device, a way to hook the reader and force them to confront their own mortality. This wasn't a comic book, and I feared the same rules didn't apply. Sebastian had proved himself to the city, to me.

Tears streamed down my cheeks. "You're a hero."

24

Sentinel held me as if I were a blushing bride. I didn't know if the other Centurions had deemed this battle worth their attention but at least Bernard had answered my plea for help. He had said nothing since he found me on the rooftop, maintaining his stoic demeanor.

He landed on the street where camera crews had already set up camp. To any onlooker, he was one of the most recognized superheroes in Vanguard, a rare sight in the Ward. Setting me down, he held onto my sleeve. I tried to jerk free, but he held up a finger, prompting me to wait.

Around his waist there were a dozen pouches holding whatever it was that superheroes might need on their adventures. He pulled out a cell phone and handed it to me.

"How long have you known?"

His cowl hid most of his face. Circles were cut out for his eyes and mouth, making his beard stand out. The leather hugged his body, emphasizing his muscles, unlike the baggy shirts he wore at brunch. As his chest rose and fell, he embodied the very epitome of a superhero. But underneath, he was still the same Bernard.

"A long time."

"You never said anything."

I shook my head. "Not my secret to tell."

Sentinel patted me on the shoulder, giving me a quick nod. He rose into the air, his cape catching in the wind.

"Go find him," he said, "I'll see what I can find from above."

Bernard launched himself upward into the sky. Seconds later he was flying deeper into the Ward, scouting for any signs of Sebastian. Before I could take another step, two news crews surrounded me.

A woman in a crisp blazer already had a microphone in hand. The male reporter didn't stand a chance as he hurried to button his jacket and snatch a mic from his assistant.

"Do you know Sentinel? Are there other Centurions in the area?" She didn't care about me, or even the battle that had transpired. She wanted footage of the heavy hitters. That type of footage could make a reporter's career.

"Is he going for reinforcements?" The man asked a question before he had his microphone ready. Neither of them were asking the right questions, and I let out a low growl. The vultures didn't take the hint and spewed another round of questions about Bernard's alter-ego.

I moved to my tiptoes, scanning about the flipped vehicles. Everywhere I turned, there was destruction, a barrage of smashed buildings, indents in the pavement, and screeching alarms the length of the block. Xander would bitch about the collateral damage, the unnecessary injuries, and the general danger of superheroes existing. This was the price we paid to be saved. Today in the Ward, it was a costly victory.

Behind their camera crews, a lone woman holding a pad of paper cleared her throat. When that didn't stop her television counterparts from speaking over one another, she shouted. "Who is the new hero?"

Both reporters quieted. She nudged her way through, getting awkwardly close. "Misty with the Beacon," she stated her credentials, despite the t-shirt proudly displaying the magazine's logo, a logo *I* made. "Wraith has been terrorizing the Ward for weeks. Who is the new hero that defeated her?"

"I—uh—his name is," I gulped. There are so many things that go into a name. This wasn't naming a newborn whom you hoped would grow into the moniker. His name would serve as his legacy, a tiny blip in the grand scheme of superheroes. It needed to embody his strength, determination, and, at the end... I suppressed the sob.

I cycled through the possible names as I met her stare. Waiting patiently, her eyes lit up, literally. A soft light spread across her face, and for a moment, I thought she might be like Sebastian.

"Hyperion."

The titan, father of Helios, the sun. Misty's eyes no longer focused on me, instead looking past me to something far more impressive. She squinted, and even then, I could see the reflection in her eyes. I didn't dare turn around, convinced the moment I laid eyes on him I'd begin weeping.

"I apologize for vanishing. But I personally needed to make sure Wraith was locked up in the station." Carefully selected words spoken for the benefit of me. "I'm told it's what heroes are supposed to do."

My heart swelled.

"You're new to the Ward. Where did you come from?" Misty didn't waste time directing the story.

"I've been here for quite some time."

"Why step into the role of hero now?"

"I," he paused. Turning slowly, I shielded my eyes. Hovering a few feet off the ground, he had limited his light, using it to skillfully hide his identity. I wanted to reach out, to run my hands along his chest, holding him tightly, confirming that he was, in-fact still alive.

"It took losing somebody important for me to get my head out of my ass." It wasn't fair. Sebastian could hide his apology in the answer to Misty's questions, but I couldn't speak without revealing my connection to him. Being on the receiving end of an apology which you can't return required more willpower than I expected.

"Hyperion, will you be the Ward's newest hero?"

"You might see me from time to time," he admitted, "but the Ward has protectors. My origin story is in South-land. I think it's time I return. There are a few bad guys there that need the shit beaten out of them."

Until that last line, I thought he had done a complete one-hundred-and-eighty degree turn. I would have called him out for telling me what I wanted to hear or changing himself for my sake. He might have assumed the mantle of a hero, but he wasn't going to don the heroic rhetoric. Somewhere between good and bad, Sebastian found his footing. Thankfully, his heart held good intent, a new layer of heroing I'd have to learn to accept.

"I have business to attend to." I hadn't noticed that his right arm remained tight across his torso. Through the shimmering light, it was impossible to see the damage, but the puddle of red forming on the cement disclosed the grave injuries.

"But if you want to know more, speak with Griffin

Smith. I can't take the credit for defeating Wraith. It was his bravery that saved me and the city. Remember, not all heroes wear capes."

With that, he flew straight up before changing direction out of the city. Was he going to get medical attention? Was there a superhero medic waiting for him? My questions were answered as I caught a sign of Sentinel speeding to catch up. Did that mean Sebastian and Bernard would know one another's secrets? Juggling identities was going to get tough, but I was glad to know that the alter egos of the surrounding men were heroes destined for greatness.

"Griffin." Misty shoved one of the reporters, trying to block her. She had no problem asserting her dominance. "First you stand up to Vincent, the scourge of the Beacon, and now a supervillain, what's next?" I wasn't surprised that the reporters at the magazine heard about my explosive departure.

I had a job waiting for me at Revelations. With Wraith being locked up, I believed the atmosphere might be less hostile. But, unfortunately, with Damien Vex in charge, pushing his anti-hero agenda, I'd be fueling a propaganda machine aimed to take down heroes like Sebastian.

"My arch nemesis hasn't been defeated, not yet."

I couldn't demand Sebastian become a hero without taking my own advice. It was time I stopped doubting my worth. I might not be able to fly, or throw cars like skipping stones, but it was time. I needed to be the hero of my own story.

"What can I do?" Misty took me by the arm, guiding me away from the asinine questions of the other two reporters. "I've always wanted to be a sidekick."

I laughed at the irony.

25

———————

"Sidekicks: The New Hero."

Mr. Bossman hemmed and hawed at his computer monitor. He had taken off his jacket, loosened his tie, preparing to end his workday and leave the office. I shouldn't have been able to walk into his office, but it paid being nice to security. Janet had handed off her keycard, and Sofia buzzed me in with a knowing smile. Misty said I had allies, but it wasn't until I saw them standing up in their cubicles, nodding their approval, that I finally believed the reporter.

"Forty-eight hours ago, I nearly died helping Hyperion save the city," I began. "Our newest hero is the reason the Beacon is still standing. Without him, your employees would be dead and your building, a pile of rubble."

"I'm not a fan of our writers going rogue and posting to the website without approval."

Misty had put her job on the line. I tried to convince her to play it safe, but she had been adamant. Not wanting to wait for the print publication, she posted the article to the Beacon's website without Bossman's approval. When she clicked the publish button, I thought I would die.

"It's a policy that should be reconsidered."

"Mr. Smith—"

"This article, in less than a day, has doubled the traffic to the Beacon. It has the highest engagement rating we've seen in years."

"We?"

Before I could respond, the door burst open. I didn't need to turn around to know Vincent had barged into the room. Janet had played her role perfectly, informing the rat I was meeting with Bossman. I flinched as the door slammed behind him. He was quick to move beside Mr. Bossman, taking up his role as the court jester.

"I'm sorry, I didn't know security let him in the building." Vincent fixed his tie, straightening out his suit so that he looked far more formal than the relaxed big boss. I wondered if the collar of his shirt hid a bruise from being pinned to the wall.

"I'll call the cops and report him for trespassing," he continued.

"Quiet." The single word from Mr. Bossman silenced

Vincent, though he looked as if he had plenty to say. I couldn't hide the grin, the satisfaction that the bootlicker had been put in his place.

"What are your terms?"

"Mr. Boss—" Vincent started.

"I want a job."

"Already jumping ship at Revelations?" He leaned forward on his desk, resting on his elbows. He might not look his usual formal self, but the magazine's owner never surrendered control of the room.

"I prefer to see the good in our heroes."

"I see."

Vincent pointed at me, sputtering as he sorted through the list of insults he had prepared. "He's trying to ransom his way back onto the magazine. This is a coup!"

"Your former position *is* still available," Mr. Bossman said.

I could swear the man's lip curled at the offer. I was prepared to accept, wiping my sweaty hand on my pants in anticipation of shaking on the deal.

"Or, are you still interested in the Art Director position?"

"Mr. Bossman! I refuse to work with this talentless hack!" Vincent sputtered.

Nobody spoke, the silence hanging in the air. I wanted to throw Vincent to the floor, maybe drive my fist into his eye. I had to remind myself to take the high road. A week ago, I would have knuckled under or doubted myself until I shook from anxiety. After staring down Wraith and emerging victorious, the Art Director hardly moved my needle.

"Good," Mr. Bossman started, "Sofia sent me security footage of the attack."

There was no way to hide my gasp. Nobody had discussed getting Vincent fired. Sofia had gone rogue. It wasn't surprising with how many people carried a grudge against the man. I imagined the assistant sitting at her desk, giggling over her victory.

"You're fired," Mr. Bossman stated sharply.

"You can't—"

"It's *my* magazine, Mr. Bailey."

Mr. Bossman stood slowly, widening his shoulders as he went. They were roughly the same height, but with his sleeves rolled, it was obvious who was the bigger of the two. Never had I seen Bossman use his physique to intimidate, but I took satisfaction in the fact Vincent stepped back.

"I can. I will. I did."

A chipper voice pipped into the room from the intercom. "Mr. Bossman, would you like to me to call security to escort our former employee from the building?"

Sofia, that girl deserved a hug, high-five, and a shot.

Vincent's jaw remained slacked, snarling at me between grumblings. He stood up straight, pretending he maintained his dignity.

"This isn't the last you've heard of me."

"We'll keep an eye out for you in the police logs," she barked from the other room.

Mr. Bossman snorted at Sofia's quip. The former employee stormed out of the room. He didn't bother slamming the door, which seemed like a missed opportunity to punctuate his dramatic departure.

"Shall I send a condolences bouquet?" Okay, Sofia would get a night of drinking for free.

"The Beacon is in your debt," Mr. Bossman began. "I'm not sure how you managed to orchestrate this display, but it's obvious you have the respect of the staff."

"Thank you." I'd be saying that a lot in the near future. My chest swelled with pride at the quick manner in which they offered to pitch in.

"Will you accept the position?"

He moved from behind the desk, standing close enough I could smell the last hints of his cologne. He held out his hand, holding it steady as I wrapped my head around the turn of events.

"If you're not—"

"Yes. I accept." I grabbed his hand with both of mine, shaking it vigorously. "This isn't how I imagined this meeting going."

"Once you left, I did my due diligence. It seems I made the mistake of letting Vincent run amok in my company. Nobody had a nice thing to say about the man, but when I asked them about you…" He freed his hand from my compulsive shaking and rested it on my shoulder. "I think it might be time to try some of these big ideas you have."

"Mr. Bossman—"

"Darrel."

This would take getting used to. "Darrel, I don't know what to say."

"You're going to need to get over that fast. I'm giving you three days to meet with the design staff. I want something fresh that is going to do these heroes justice. Since Misty has taken a liking to you," he laughed, "no easy feat, I assure you. You'll need to set up a meeting with her for the feature article for this reveal."

"What's the feature?"

I had always found the man to be intimidating. He ran the magazine like a business and often that meant he didn't understand the artistry behind creating a publication. But as he leaned against his desk, the smiling stretching across his face, he transformed into a guy I might invite out to have a drink and talk about life beyond the office.

"I love a good origin story. I hear there's a new hero in Southlands making a name for himself. I thought the Beacon's star sidekick might be able to get us an interview."

"I can do that." After date night, of course.

EPILOGUE 1

Sebastian's text hadn't given any details. This new mysterious side of him left me grinning, but it meant dressing for date night had been a challenge. I hadn't seen him since he defeated Wraith, and decided to play it cool. T-shirt with a superhero logo and jeans. As I stood in front of the burger joint in Southland, I realized he crafted tonight just for me.

"Sly bastard."

It wasn't a big restaurant, a few high-top tables and a couple of booths off to the side. Searching for his signature tailor suit, I missed him on first inspection. When he stood from the booth, a t-shirt with a picture of the Centurions and jeans, I had to keep from audibly swooning.

I didn't know what to expect. Our last encounter as

Griffin and Sebastian had been explosive. My anxiety washed away as he charged, throwing his arms around me. The kiss that followed pushed away my doubts. His stubble scratched against my chin, and I had to remind myself we were in a public place. Even then, I thought about tossing him on a table and tearing the clothes off his body.

"It's endearing when I wear one," I pointed to my shirt, "it's shameless marketing when you do it."

"I was worried you might not come."

There were lingering emotions from our fight, but I wanted to squash those before we took our seats. "I said some horrible stuff. I..." My cheeks burned from embarrassment.

"No," he whispered the word. "I needed somebody to jostle my perspective. I needed... What I'm trying to say... I mean..." Sebastian nervous might be my new favorite version of the man.

"I need my sidekick." He took my hand, giving it a strong squeeze, a fraction of the strength hidden behind those bulging muscles. "I want to play Legos with you."

Jesus. Shots had been fired, and they struck my heart with a bang. No, not a bang, a thermonuclear blast. I returned the squeeze. At a loss for words, I relied on my eyes and determined grin to relay the emotion bubbling in my chest.

A waitress walked up to the two of us, holding large white plates. Her white and blue checkered dress reminded me of an old diner, and it dawned on me how hard Sebastian attempted to reach me on my level.

"You gentlemen going to eat food or are you skipping right to dessert?"

We slid into the booth, and she set down the plates. Her name tag read, "Mildred," and it couldn't have been more perfect. She gave me a light pat on the shoulder, "You'll need your energy for later."

As she walked away, Sebastian laughed at my slack jaw and wide eyes. "She's a firecracker. Been slinging burgers since I was a kid."

"So how have you been?"

"You know," he chomped away at a fry, "I've been great."

"I was worried after..." I let the rest of the statement hang in the air. "You could have called." I wasn't annoyed, but when you see the man you... admire, stabbed, there is a certain amount of worry.

"I'm not very good at this." He reached across the table, sliding his fingers over my hand. "I didn't know what to say. Sorry for being an arrogant jerk? Sorry for not being your ideal guy?"

"Yeah, I deserve that."

"Couples have growing pains," he leaned in to whisper, "ours just happen to be of super proportions. I didn't want to have this conversation and make promises about changing. You deserve better than that. That's the reason I came back to Southland."

"Wait, all of this," I refused to cry over a cheeseburger, "for me?"

"Sorry it's not flowers or chocolate."

He casually returned to his French fries. I laughed hard enough that my stomach rumbled, and my jaw hurt. The one other table with people stopped and stared, and at that point, I just didn't care. Who needs flowers when your boyfriend was willing to put away villains in your honor? For a comic book loving geek, there was no better present.

The conversation slowed as we stuffed our faces. I don't know if it was the burger or the company, but it could have very well been the best meal I had ever eaten. I'd have to make sure Mildred paid my compliments to the cook.

Along the wall, there were dozens of posters for upcoming performances from the local theater and music venues. When people thought of Southland, they tended to focus on the crime statistics and poverty ratings, myself included. But as I caught sight of a gallery opening, my opinion quickly changed.

"We'll need to check out that gallery show."

"Sounds like a follow-up date to me."

"Not a follow-up," I wiped the ketchup from my lips, "just the first of many."

"I need to ask you something." His tone turned serious, almost quiet. My heart jumped to my throat, worried that a perfect date was about to go south.

"Yeah?"

"I've never done this before, but this," he pointed back and forth between him and me, "us. It's a thing, right?"

"Did you just ask to make this official?"

"You're going to make me say it, aren't you?"

His cheeks turned red, and he struggled to maintain eye contact. Seeing him bashful had been rare, and I savored every moment of it.

"Yup."

He gave a dramatic sigh. "This is harder than taking down Dino Destruction."

"I'm in no rush." Okay, maybe it was a bit mean not giving him a helping hand. But, some part of me loved the buildup.

"I want this to be a thing."

Okay, now it was just cruel. "Exclusive? Boyfriends? Partners?"

"Thank you!" He sucked in a deep breath. "I'm working on it, I swear."

"Boyfriend," I whispered the word. It had been a long time since somebody earned that title. I watched as my boyfriend finished his burger. A dab of mustard hung on his lip before he grabbed a napkin and wiped down his face. I don't know if it was the newly assumed mantle, or it was him in a superhero t-shirt devouring a burger, but I was happy. Genuinely, truthfully, happy.

Mildred appeared as if by magic, scooping up our plates. The moment she vanished, Sebastian's gaze turned mischievous. He transformed from the scared man into that cocky designer I first bumped into at the Beacon.

"Do you trust me?"

"I think so?" Where was he going with this?

"Follow me." With that, he slapped money on the table and took me by the hand, guiding me outside.

"I have a surprise for you."

Heaven help me.

"If this is you taking your clothes off," I laughed, "I've seen it all before."

"Don't peek." Sebastian's voice relayed a mix of child-like vigor and adamancy. He had me planted in the middle of his mid-century modern sofa while he ducked into the bedroom. I expected to smell cologne, or body wash from the bathroom, but his apartment remained freakishly clean. We'd have to work on that, otherwise he'd never let me spend the night.

"Can I open—"

"Don't make me blind you."

"Yes, daddy."

"You know I can throw you half way across the city, right?"

I snickered.

For the last three days, Sebastian had gone out of his

way to prove he held the heart of a hero. There were no speeches promising he'd change in the future. He had gone with the grand gesture approach. A series of drug busts, aiding elderly women, and photo op with a Girl Scout troop had filled my heart, and all as a demonstration for me. Reality had fallen apart, and I found myself in a super-hero driven romantic comedy.

"Eyes closed?"

"If you're not wearing a jock strap, I'm going to be..." The door opened, and it was quite possibly the only thing more amazing than this muscular man in his underwear.

"Don't laugh. I feel a bit ridiculous."

Sebastian stood in the doorway, shifting uncomfortably in a skintight suit. While the majority of it was black, the chest in a downward facing V stood out in a brilliant white. I wanted to whistle or make a snarky comment, but I realized that Hyperion's outfit had been copied from my painting.

"The Centurion techs had to take some liberties for my abilities."

"It's perfect." My words were breathy as I struggled to shove my heart back into my chest. Instead of running through the airport to confess his undying love, he'd taken a dream and made it a reality.

As he walked toward the couch, his powers erupted, breaking through thin transparent strips of his costume. Even the chest piece lit up as if he were a human beacon.

"Thank you," he said. He held out his hand, and as I placed my hand in his, he pulled me to my feet, then off my feet. Hugging me tight against his chest, we slowly spun in a circle. He could thank me all day long, but this origin story belonged to the both of us.

I brushed a bit of hair away from his face before kissing him. Cupping the sides of his head, I bit down on his lower lip, teasing him enough that he reached down grabbing my ass. It quickly went from playful to lustful. I needed his weight on top of me as he fucked me.

"I hope you can get out of the suit faster than you put it on."

"Oh?"

I pulled back and his raised eyebrow transitioned into a wide-eyed stare. We stopped rotating and touched down. As I pulled my t-shirt over my head, he was already peeling the suit off his body. By the time I unzipped my jeans, he was standing stark naked, and I had to slow to take in the sight of him.

"Follow me." I took him by the hand and headed toward his bedroom. As we walked into the dark room, he threw a glowing orb above the bed, where it cast a soft light across the room. Atop his dresser sat a Lego replica of a spaceship from Star Wars, a sign that I found a keeper.

Before I could turn around, he gave me a push, sending me onto all fours on the geometric patterned comforter. I could feel him step between my legs. I imagined his cock pressed against my ass and, just like that, I was hard as a rock. As much as I wanted him to shove inside, at his size, lube was required, and even then it'd be a rough ride.

His fingers grazed my calves, dragging along my skin until he reached my thighs. As he changed direction, following my skin upward, I shivered. Knowing he could hurl a car made the gentle caress even more erotic. I wanted him to fuck me, but I didn't want this to stop.

A single finger traced a line down the middle of my ass. I gasped, and then again as it reached the underside of my sack. It turned to a moan as he reached under, running his hand along my cock. I pushed back, signaling for him to pick up the pace. What can I say, I can be a pushy bottom.

He shifted his weight. The light touch turned firm as he gripped my ass in both hands. He squeezed hard enough that I'd have a handprint sized bruise on my ass in the morning. I'd gripe, but I loved a morning after reminder.

"Oh fuck." The stubble of his chin pressed against my taint, and suddenly, every nerve along my skin fired. It started with a flick of the tongue. Teasing, I desperately tried to push back, but his hands held me in place. Sebastian made it clear, tonight he was in control.

I clenched the comforter as his teasing turned to vigorous licking. His hands slid from my ass to my hips as he pulled me back, burying his tongue. If he wanted to drive me wild, he already achieved that goal.

"Fuck me." I meant it to be filled with yearning, almost begging, but it came out as a command.

"Yes, sir," he whispered, kissing my inner thigh.

For the size of his cock, I should have let him continue rimming, but patience wasn't a virtue I possessed. As he stood, he pressed himself against my ass, reminding me of his thickness. He stepped back for a moment and the familiar sounds of spit coating an erection filled the space between my panting.

My fingers curled around the fabric, bracing for the pleasure coated in pain. As he resumed his position between my legs, I could feel the head of his hard-on demanding entry. The first inch pushed inside and I buried my face in the bed, moaning loud enough to give the neighbors alarm.

My lack of frequent bottoming would have made an average penis feel huge, but when Sebastian entered, it pushed me to my limits. Thankfully, Sebastian held still, giving me a chance to adjust to his girth. Meanwhile, he continued the light touches along my legs, a reminder that he was focused on my comfort.

For the next minute, we didn't move as I forced my body to relax, to accept him. Lust overtook common sense, and I rocked back and forth, each time gasping as more of his dick slid inside. Now it was his turn to moan. With hands firmly planted on my hips, he pulled me back until I could feel his balls brush against mine.

We both froze, savoring the sensation.

"You're so damned thick." To mock my comment, he flexed his penis, causing it to jump. I groaned at the thickness stretching my ass to its limits.

It turned amazing as he started with slow strokes. The sounds coming out of my mouth could only be described as whimpers. I was at Sebastian's mercy. I went for my own cock to feel the trail of wetness, but he reached around my waist, firmly gripping the length of my shaft. Each time he thrust, he shoved me forward, jerking me off.

"Don't stop." Now I begged.

His hips gyrated like a professional. Once I grew accustomed to his girth, he pulled himself all the way out and before I could beg, he slammed the entire length inside. Leaning over my body, he wrapped an arm around my waist and pulled me onto my side, with him molded to my back. The sensation bordered on overwhelming, his entire body touching mine while he returned to the fast jabs.

"Want me to cum?" It was a courtesy question, and as I reached back, hand on his ass urging him deeper, he had his answer.

His mouth rested next to my ear, where I could hear the shallow breathing like a storm. "I'm close." I dug my nails into his ass. His pace quickened as he let out a low growl.

The orb above us flared and shattered. Tiny dots of light showered down around us like fireworks. "I'm — argh." His rhythm faltered, and he bit down on my shoulder as he howled. I closed my eyes, savoring the jerking of his cock as he came inside me.

I could have fallen asleep there, with him still buried in my ass.

Sebastian had another finale in mind.

He continued a slow rocking, using his cum as lube. Wrapping his hand around my erection, he used the skin to jerk me off. I leaned my head back while he continued kissing my neck. His cock hadn't softened, and he persisted with his slow fuck.

My body went rigid as the electrifying sensation pulsed from my groin, flooding my body. In the dark of his bedroom, he moved quickly, pulling himself free and sliding down the length of the bed. He rolled me onto my back, barely wrapping his lips around the head of my dick before I came.

There was no shyness, as I pushed his head down, burying myself in his throat. I groaned, letting the waves of pleasure wash over my body. I could feel his throat massage my shaft as he swallowed every drop. He scored technical points in the sack for pulling off that maneuver.

"Damn," I gasped.

I removed my hand, letting him up to gasp for air. He spent the next few minutes lapping up my cum, ensuring he hadn't missed a stray drop. I finally had to push him away as I turned sensitive.

He moved up the bed, sliding behind me. Apparently,

the taste of cum left his motor running, as I could feel his stiffness slide between the cheeks of my ass. Maybe if he gave me a half hour to recharge, I'd crawl on top of him and start round two.

"That was amazing." He kissed down the back of my neck, tucking his body against mine. Despite having cum less than a minute ago, his erection hadn't softened.

"Yes, it was." I pulled his arm across my chest. As the little spoon, a guy wants to feel protected, as if the big spoon will do anything to keep them safe. Most people didn't have a big spoon who could punch through concrete. First the position at the Beacon—oh crap. I had forgotten Darrel's insistence on featuring Hyperion in the magazine.

"Stay the night?" he asked sheepishly, as if I might say no.

"I'll say yes on one condition."

"Anything." He continued kissing across my shoulder blades.

"Hyperion agrees to an appearance at the Beacon."

"Wait, what?"

"Thanks," I gave his hand a squeeze, "I appreciate it."

Sebastian grumbled about the separation of personal and professional as he thumped his head against the pillow in a huff. My eyelids grew heavy as I replayed the scene in the office where I first met him. From the moment I eyed this dashing man, there had been chemistry. While it had a bumpy beginning, the ending turned out magical. Right now, in his arms, I had never felt more at home.

I couldn't have predicted a chance encounter would develop into a love story... a superhero love story.

And yet, here we were...

EPILOGUE 2

"Jesus, you *are* in love," Lydia said, pointing at the papers on her counter.

Her hair must have measured over a foot, split into two identical, fiery red pigtails. The mention of the word love coming from the woman wearing all black and a t-shirt depicting a man severing the head of a zombie bordered on comical.

"You don't like it?"

"Whoa. Whoa." She held up her hand as she inspected the dozen pages on the counter. "I didn't say that." While being the Art Director for the Beacon let me flex my design muscles, I had finally relented and agreed to work on a comic with Lydia. Filled with action, espionage, and superheroes hunted by the government, I felt the need to sneak in a moment of romance in our plot.

"But adding hearts above Dante's head? He just slaughtered the henchmen of his nemesis. He's covered in blood." She paused and eyed it again. Lydia's face contorted this way and that, as if she were trying to find the expression that matched the twisted thoughts inside that beautiful brain of hers. "I take it all back. I love it. If I just slaughtered the lackeys of my greatest rival, I'd probably have little hearts above my head, too."

"You were right." Sebastian stepped up to the counter with at least forty comics. "She's my kind of people."

Defeated. My boyfriend and creative partner were never allowed to hang out together. We might need to establish the comic book shop as office limits. If he could forbid me from going to the drug kingpin's delicatessen, home of the world's best roast beef sandwich, I could ban him from my local comic shop. It was essentially the same thing.

"Damn," she laughed, "he even looks like you." Holding up the comic book page, she closed one eye and compared Sebastian to Dante's love interest. There was no denying it, I'd gladly spend my days drawing Sebastian, especially if he insisted on staying in briefs when spending the night.

He awkwardly thrust the arm full of comics toward Lydia. After reciting comic books to him during every training session, he insisted on coming with me for the sake of research. At first he gave me grief for comparing him to the caped crusaders in comics. It'd be sweet if he were taking an interest, but I think he wanted them as study material. Next would be him practicing punchy tag lines every time he did something cool with his powers.

"Griffin, I'm blaming you for his bad taste in reading material." She tossed several of them on the far side of the counter. "No. Trash. No. No. The artwork is tolerable." By the time she finished going through his stack and ringing them up, there couldn't be more than ten left.

"You really have a thing for men in spandex." Her attention turned to me. "Looks like you're not the only hero chaser, Griff."

"Wouldn't it make more sense to sell them all to me?" Sebastian questioned.

"Griffin," she pointed at me, her finger attempting to tear from her hand and jab me in the chest. "Check yo' man."

I let out a long sigh. "Lydia isn't a comic book shop owner. She's a graphic novel reading list curator. She has a higher calling."

"But the sales?" Sebastian was adorable as he tried to make sense of the nonsensical.

"She's loaded."

"Am not," she argued.

"Failed business school. Bought a comic shop."

"You diminish my public service."

I shot her a smile. "Lydia has never lived the Ramen lifestyle."

"I have—" She scowled at me. "Okay, you got me. It's true."

I expected Sebastian to turn sour at the mention of her being one of the rich. His disdain for the upper class had popped up several times, but he acknowledged his bias. Sometimes, he even managed to surprise me.

He eyed the digital readout on the register. Pulling out his credit card, he slid it through the machine. "The Goddess of Graphics," he winked at her, "I can get behind that."

"Careful, or I'll propose." Lydia bagged the comics and handed them to Sebastian. "So, when are you going to finish the colored pages? The publisher wants to add this to the fall line-up."

"I need to go next door and get inks from Clarice."

Sebastian offered a wave as he waited by the door. Lydia attempted to play coy and blow him a kiss. The moment he was out of earshot, the geeky anarchist leaned across the counter, pulling at my t-shirt until I was only inches from her face.

"I love him. If I'm not your flower girl, I'll slash your tires."

"No car."

"Murder your house plants."

"Already dead."

"I'm not playing, Smith. I want a cute dress and rose petals, dammit."

We had only been dating for a few weeks, but I'd be lying if I hadn't thought about the possibility. I never imagined being in a relationship again, and here I was, thinking about Sebastian in a tuxedo. It might be the only thing sexier than his superhero costume. Either way, they'd be on the floor before the end of the night.

"I'll consider it."

"Speaking of sexy men," she pulled out her phone. "You got a photo of Hyperion? I can't believe you're beating my score." Clicking on my profile, she pulled up my photographs. I knew the photo well. Hyperion hovering over a cop car holding two bank robbers by their belts. Minutes after it had been taken, the Southland chief of police officially thanked the hero for his dedication to the neglected borough.

"Took me forever. Now I want to get one of that lady that walks through walls." I neglected to mention she had approached Sebastian about working together to topple a crime syndicate operating in the city.

"I'm going to become a vigilante so I can photograph myself. You're not going to win." She let go of my shirt, patting it, trying to smooth out the wrinkles left by her talons. Lydia might be joking, but half the heroes in comics were rich people with too much free time. Spite made people do crazy things.

We said our farewells, and Sebastian held the door open as I exited. Walking toward the Art Supply Store, he let his pinky wrap around mine, a subtle gesture that had almost become a requirement as we walked. I pulled my hand free, looping around his, leaning on the man as we approached the red wooden door of the store.

"Don't let me forget the flowers," he said, holding the door open.

Slipstream proved more of a fighter than we could have anticipated. It was Xander who kept her alive long enough to be taken to the Centurion's headquarters. The heroine wouldn't be saving the city in the near future, but Sebastian assured me she'd make a full recovery.

"Flowers?" I mouthed. Forget dying plants. That woman deserved a puppy.

Once we were inside, Sebastian's eyes glazed over. If we were shopping for wine, or looking for vacation rentals, he'd have plenty to say. He might have an eye for the arts, but he had always focused on the commercial side of the profession. Between the comic book shop and the art store, he had entered my domain. I appreciated that he abandoned his comfort zone to spend the day with me.

"So this is where you spend your Thursday evenings." If I was going to work on the comic, my art skills needed a refresher. Clarice had proven to be a wonderful teacher, both in drawing and painting.

Clarice walked down the paint aisle, arms outstretched. "I'm doing a wheel throwing class in the future. You should join." With a peck on the cheek, her face lit up at the sight of Sebastian. "You must be the boyfriend." She repeated the hug and kiss on the cheek.

"I could be persuaded," he said, winking at me.

"Your inks came in this morning. Give me a few minutes. I need to find the box in the back. Treat the store like home."

Before I could reply, she had already passed the turpentine and headed toward the easels. "She's quirky, but she's an amazing teacher."

"I see that."

I followed Sebastian's eye line to a painting hanging on the wall. She created a display of her students' work, mine hanging in the middle of the wall. I had left the work with Clarice, hoping to work on it a bit longer before gifting it to Sebastian.

"Surprise." I stepped next to him, taking his hand and squeezing it between my palms. "It was *supposed* to be a gift."

Seconds dragged on as he stared at the canvas. It had him dressed in his costume, producing rays of light from his exposed skin. The almost comic book style depicted Hyperion tearing away shadows, vanquishing the surrounding darkness. It had been the emergence of a new hero, and as much as I painted it for Sebastian, I needed to see that moment frozen in time.

"Why this scene?" His words were soft. "Why this fight?"

"To me, it's when you became a hero." It was partially the truth, but when he squeezed my hand, I couldn't hold back. "This is where my doubts about us evaporated." It was closer to the full explanation; the emotional undercurrent I didn't dare say without getting mushy.

Sebastian leaned his head on my shoulder, snaking a hand around my waist. One moment we'd be tangled in one another, and the next he'd return to that rigid man. He was trying, and with every act, I—

"That moment is when I knew," I confessed.

"Knew?" He was going to make me say it.

He had spent the last hour roaming through a comic book store as I talked to Lydia. Sebastian let me control the television remote at night and watch horrible sci-fi movies. When I had a tough day at work, he'd cook breakfast for dinner or put on music and made me dance away my woes. He made the happy moments more joyful and the sad ones, he held my hand while I worked my way through them. Sebastian deserved the truth.

"It's the moment I knew I loved you."

"That long, huh? I knew the moment you turned your back and stormed off that day in front of Revelations."

"Our fight is when you knew?" It seemed like an odd moment to discover you loved somebody.

"The moment you turned around, I saw what I was about to lose. My chest hurt. If I was going to be heartbroken..." He turned around, facing me so our foreheads touched. "I don't know when I fell in love with you. But I knew it was love at that moment."

I closed my eyes and gave him a gentle kiss.

"I love you," I whispered.

"I know," he replied.

Wait, did he just... I pulled back to a shit-eating grin stapled on his face.

"You did not just quote Star Wars..."

— The End —

Follow Xander's Story in
Men of Vanguard Book 2:
Infernal Justice

Want More Men of Vanguard?
Join Ryder's Scandalous Super's Newsletter

AFTERWORD

I am a gay man obsessed with superheroes. As a kid, I had no role models, and that hasn't changed much as an adult. Because of this, I bringing my relationships, sex life, and love of comics to the forefront in the *Men of Vanguard Series*. The characters in these books reflect personal experiences and themes set against a fictional backdrop.

ABOUT THE AUTHOR

Superheroes stories are at core of Ryder O'Malley's origin story. Refusing to read as a child, everything changed with the first stack of comics. He has always been a fan of forbidden romances within the pages of comics. It should be expected that he'd turn around and start writing his own stories filled with sexy, super, man-on-man action. Ryder's novels draw on his own experiences as a gay man in search of love.

Ryder lives in Boston, Massachusetts and will soon be making the trek to Glasgow, Scotland to join his long-time partner and live his happily-ever-after. When he's not writing, he can be found working on client book covers (which means he's admiring the abs of muscular men with a little bit of chest hair.)